A MADE IN JERSEY NOVEL

WORKED *Up*

A MADE IN JERSEY NOVEL

WORKED
Up

TESSA BAILEY

Entangled Publishing, LLC
2614 South Timberline Road
Suite 105, PMB 159
Fort Collins, CO 80525
rights@entangledpublishing.com

·   Brazen is an imprint of Entangled Publishing, LLC.

Edited by Heather Howland
Cover design by Heather Howland
Cover photo by Sara Eirew, featuring Daria Rottenberk and Garrett
Pentecost

Manufactured in the United States of America

First Edition August 2016

ENTANGLED
BRAZEN

Dear Reader,

Really, I have Pinterest to thank for this book. For Duke's character, mainly. Over a year and a half ago, I found a picture of a greased up mechanic with a pissed off demeanor on Pinterest and I named him Duke, having no idea when/if I would be able to write him. And then along came Pouty Man Bear (#PMB). For those unaware, I have a Facebook group called Bailey's Babes and every once in a while, I get inspired by a plot bunny SO BADLY, I have no choice but to ride it out. The Babes let me drop installments on them at random times and rejoice along with me. Pouty Man Bear was a five-installment chronicle of a big, bearded, NYC baker who had some extra cushion for the pushin' and grumbled. A lot. We all *adored* this mountain of man meat and it just so happens, I was writing Duke's book at the same time and was definitely inspired by the chronicle. So, I hope everyone enjoyed *this* #PMB in all his glory. Thank you, Pinterest gods.

For Pouty Man Bears Everywhere
We Salute You
#PMB

Chapter One

It was the type of place Samantha Waverly usually avoided.

Precisely why she was going in.

As always, when Sam encountered a dose of inconvenient nerves—a frequent occurrence of late—she reached into her brown leather satchel and ran a thumb over the spiraling metal holding her sketchpad together. By the end of summer, she'd have calluses on top of her existing calluses. Ones wrought by hours of holding pencils and charcoal. Or *joy wounds*, as she secretly referred to them, since they'd been formed doing what she loved. Drawing.

The urge to whip out her sketchpad and illustrate the dilapidated bar across the street was fierce, but night had fallen and standing by herself in the strange neighborhood of Hook, New Jersey too long didn't seem wise. What was the name of the bar? She squinted through the darkness at the worn, unlit sign. THE THIRD SHIFT.

Lordy, the place was a dive. Even an inexperienced bar patron, such as herself, knew the neon bar signs were relics from the eighties. The music followed suit, a young Springsteen crooning about being born to run from inside the small establishment, masculine voices chanting along, occasionally stopping to cheer, presumably at the baseball game also being played at full volume, loud enough that Samantha could hear it thirty yards away.

She just prayed their air conditioning worked. Beneath her feet, the concrete still retained the day's excessive warmth, making her shift side to side in her sandals. After the mere five-block jaunt from the bus station, sweat already beaded her forehead, humidity curling the ends of her hair.

The busted door opened and slapped shut, two men in cut off T-shirts splitting a match to light their cigarettes. One nudged the other, both of their attention cutting to where she stood.

"Who's 'at?" one called.

Who's that? It was the kind of question one asked when one was acquainted with every single soul in town and expected to know *her*, too, as soon as she stepped from the shadows. From what little her stepbrother, Renner, had told her about Hook, the majority of its residents had been born at the local hospital and rarely, if ever, left town. Samantha, on the other hand, only had the weekend. An unexpected turn of events.

She'd been one bus stop away from Hook when the text from Renner hit her phone. *Negotiations have been extended. Won't be in Jersey until Monday. Make yourself comfortable at the apartment.* Frankly, she'd been relieved instead of irritated. Anything to put off the meeting with Renner, the man she considered her closest family member. So close, she'd stopped calling him her stepbrother long ago, referring to him only as "brother." That closeness hadn't saved her stomach from being tied into knots on the ride from Manhattan. And the combination of having them loosened, while landing in such an unfamiliar place…made Samantha feel like stretching her legs a little.

Or a lot. Depending on your definition of stretching. Samantha's life was her job and she loved, adored, *celebrated* her fulfilling profession as a children's book illustrator. Colors and shapes flitted through her mind, sending tingles to her fingers. She'd filled every corner of her life with work, and she preferred it that way. After all, drawing, unlike people, couldn't abandon you when the going got tough.

She might never cross paths with anyone in Hook again after this. Maybe that possibility accounted for the excitement prickling up her spine.

She'd left the bright lights of Manhattan for adventure… in the sleepy factory town of Hook. Ironic, sure. But to Samantha, it made perfect sense.

Curling her right hand around the strap of her satchel, she trudged across the street, lifting a tentative hand to wave at the smokers. Maybe if she pretended she belonged, they would just go with it. "It's just me. Sam."

The men traded a glance. "Sam who?"

"Antha." No reaction. "Sam-antha," she mumbled, sliding into the bar. Apparently she couldn't be in a new town longer than ten minutes without earning her usual reputation for bad jokes.

Hoping her embarrassment would subside once inside the loud, anonymous bar, Samantha cleared the threshold… and saw that dream crumble. She was given no time to savor the cool wall of air inside The Third Shift, before every head in the place turned in her direction.

"Who's 'at?" someone asked, just above the din of baseball and Springsteen.

Forcing her shoulders back, Samantha scoped a seat at the bar and made a beeline for the rickety stool. She climbed onto the creaking wood, satchel hugged tight in her lap. With her head down, she could see perspiration rolling down her chest and disappearing into her cleavage—courtesy of the heat wave bearing down on the Northeast—and rifled through her bag for tissues. When she located them, she shot the other patrons a look, praying they'd gone back to their conversations and she could mop up her sweat in relative privacy. No such luck. Everyone still stared at Samantha over their beer bottles, men and women alike. Not in a hostile way. More in a did-an-alien-spaceship-just-land-outside kind of way.

"What'cha havin'?"

She started, losing her grip on the tissue packet, which hit the floor with a *smack*, her attention flying to the older gentleman behind the bar. *The bartender, Sam.* "Um. Er—" Her gaze fell to the closest glass sitting on the bar, property of the woman to her right. "I'll have one of those...a martini..."

"Olive or twist?"

A laugh trickled past Samantha's lips, but the bartender only cocked an eyebrow.

"What's funny?"

His hard tone had Sam shifting in her seat. "You know that joke. Charles Dickens walks into a bar..." She swallowed hard when the man only stared. "A-And the bartender asks if he'd like an olive or twist—"

The older man walked away before Samantha was finished explaining. Feeling a flush rise clear to her hairline, she attempted to hide the dangling sentence with a cough, but if the sympathetic glance from her seat neighbor was an indication, she'd had no success. *Okay.* New tactic.

Samantha slid off her seat to retrieve the dropped tissues, staying hidden way longer than necessary. "Come on," she whispered. "You're a twenty-five-year-old woman in a bar. Stop telling stupid jokes and you'll have a chance of appearing normal." Nodding once for good measure, she straightened— and whacked her head on the bar. "Son of a bitch."

Melting back into her seat, trying desperately to pretend there wasn't a throb at her right temple, Samantha took a long sip from the rim of her martini. And so it was through blurry vision and bluebirds circling her head that Samantha saw Goliath.

Were her eyes playing games with her? She closed the left one, trying to narrow her vision from double to single, but Goliath remained, the width of his shoulders taking up two seat lengths on the opposite end of the bar. If she weren't watching closely, she would never have believed how the wood actually sagged beneath his elbows as he leaned forward…watching her? Watching *her*.

A drop of sweat slid down between her breasts. She heard, felt, sensed the drop of moisture absorb into the material of her bra. The slow motion glide of it caused a quickening sensation in her stomach, and suddenly, there was no baseball or classic rock. Just her breath, her heartbeat. The large man pinning her under a look, making the air conditioner useless for all the heat generated by his…interest.

Could she even call it that? He wasn't smiling, was giving no indication he planned to approach her. And *ho-boy*, that was a definite frown moving over his craggy features. Yes, *craggy*. He wasn't a good-looking man. Nope, he was not. He resembled a villain from a gladiator movie. The one everyone fears and who never gets beaten…until the underdog steps in and saves mankind, standing over the fallen behemoth while dust settles around them.

Samantha had removed her sketchpad and a pencil from the satchel before her brain registered the action. *Draw him.* She had to draw him. Just the bare bones, so she could fill in the rest later, when she got back to Renner's place. Angling her body so the surface of her pad couldn't be viewed by the surrounding patrons, Samantha outlined Goliath, shading his cheeks to indicate the blood of his enemies. She penciled in battle armor, leather crisscrossing his barrel chest, so tight the straps risked snapping in half with one swing of his sword. *He would have hair beneath that leather…hair everywhere.* The thought made something unexpected sink in her belly.

Right. Add the hair later.

Unfortunately, the same hot slide occurred below the belt when she moved the pencil to form his thighs. Sturdy, rough-hewn legs. Big enough to support two people with no resulting exertion…

A glance from beneath her eyelashes made Samantha aware of Goliath's change in demeanor. He still frowned, but not at her. At someone behind her. *More* than one someone, it sounded like. Were they talking to her? When someone tapped Samantha on the shoulder, she shoved the sketchpad into her bag and looked back. Two toothy grins greeted her. They were attached to the men she'd passed on the way in, and while part of Samantha wished they'd leave her in peace with her sketchpad, another part hoped one of her jokes had finally charmed someone.

"So, Sam-*antha.* Haven't seen you in here before."

Behind her, Samantha heard a glass hit the bar. "Can we buy you that drink?"

"Uhhh." She glanced at the woman beside her for help but only got an amused shrug before her potential ally went back to watching baseball. What did it mean when someone accepted a drink from a man in a bar? Would she be obligated to have a conversation with them? What if they asked her to list her top five favorite Springsteen songs? She could only name two. "I guess—"

"All right, you two knuckleheads." A new voice joined the scene, reminding her of a rusty anchor being dragged up the side of an ancient boat. "Fuck off."

• • •

Unbelievable. First, Duke couldn't get a damn moment of peace in his house, now his only refuge, The Third Shift, had been invaded. Was it so much to ask in life for a sporting event to go uninterrupted by a woman? Granted, the doe-eyed brunette hadn't *asked* for his assistance—and she was a far cry from the four sisters terrorizing his household indefinitely—but an interruption was an interruption, no matter how you sliced it.

He couldn't help but notice this particular disruption was...pretty. Too pretty for him. Not that her appearance mattered one way or another to Duke. Facts were facts, though. She had a way of moving. Long, graceful moves that ran smack into uncertainty. As if she kept forming courses of action only to change her mind halfway through the execution stage. Ask him why he'd taken the time to form such a detailed observation and his answer probably wouldn't make much sense. Unfortunately, noticing her way of operating had led to...*other* observations. Impolite ones that would've surrounded the freckles on her cheeks with pink instead of flawless ivory.

Good thing he wasn't looking for a woman. Not for one night. Not for nothing.

With resolve firm in his mind, Duke focused on the problem at hand. Namely, the issue distracting him from America's game. The two men harassing Doe Eyes were machinery mechanics who worked under him at the factory, and after his brief directive to *fuck off*, they wasted no time shuffling away, beer bottles held up like little white flags.

"Sorry, Duke."

"No problem, Duke."

He grunted, watching them enviously as they rejoined their friends in front of the giant flat-screen. At least *someone* would get to watch baseball now, huh? As for him, he appeared to be stuck. For as long as Doe Eyes graced The Third Shift with her not-from-around-here presence, that is. Because if it wasn't the knuckleheads looking to purchase her drinks, it would be someone else. And after he'd watched her flounder over a simple drink order and whack her noggin on the bar, he figured she deserved some peace and quiet.

Which she would get, so long as she let him watch the motherloving game.

Duke grabbed the closest stool, flipping it around and repositioning it behind Doe Eyes. Trying not to wince over the loud creaking as he climbed on, Duke crossed his arms and went back to watching the game, bottle of Bud in hand.

He should have known the silence wouldn't last. It never did.

"Did you just…set yourself up as a roadblock?"

Duke grimaced into a sip of beer. *Damn*. She just had to have a sexy voice to match the smooth, tidy curves of her figure. He didn't want to notice…but as she spoke her tits swelled against the dress's neckline, still dewy from being outside in the high temperature, and heat trailed like fingertips down his belly. "Seems that way."

She opened her mouth to speak then shut it—damn near ten times—before finally addressing him again. "You're being very presumptuous, Duke." Her drink remained untouched on the bar. "Do you do this type of thing often?"

"Nope."

As if she'd misplaced something, she glanced in several directions, including toward the ceiling. "Should I be flattered?"

Duke had four divorcee sisters living under his roof at the moment, so he knew goddamn well when the subject needed to be changed. "What were you doing earlier? In that book of yours."

Her hesitation was brief. "Sketching you as an evil gladiator villain."

The bottle of Bud paused halfway to Duke's mouth. Wasn't every day someone caught him off guard, but this pretty girl whose voice oozed education, this girl with the stubborn—and...fuck it, *cute*—nose, had unsettled his stomach ever since gliding into the bar. Like a bad omen. He should go back to his end of the bar and stop feeding this unusual curiosity she'd inspired. Yeah, that's exactly what he should do. "Show me."

Or not.

She chewed her upper lip a beat then straightened her shoulders, pressing those perspiration-slick tits against the already-stressed buttons of her dress. For one fleeting moment, the fog of arousal enveloped his brain, making him wonder if his command of *show me* had been misinterpreted. For the love of everything holy, this—*this*—was his worst nightmare. Sprouting wood in The Third Shift during a baseball game like some horny kid ordering his first beer.

As Doe Eyes rooted through her bag for the book, Duke did something for the first time in his life. He watched the game without really seeing it. The effort to keep his gaze off her jiggling breasts and pressed-together knees as she went through the bag garnered all his concentration, blurring the action on the screen like it was happening under a foot of water. When she finally pulled the book out, Duke slowly returned his attention to her, watching her down the neck of his Bud as he sipped.

"Would you say you offend easily?"

Mouth full of beer, Duke shook his head.

Still, she hesitated. "Really I didn't even get started—"

"Let's see it." When she bristled at his tone, Duke sighed, knowing he needed a new tactic if he wanted his curiosity appeased. "What's your name?"

"It's Samantha."

Now, why the hell did her name make his cock feel chafed inside the denim of his jeans? Somehow it did, though. Made him think of her naked on dark blue, silk sheets, high heels dangling off her toes before falling, knocked free by a man's thrusts. His. *Goddammit*, this wasn't convenient whatsoever. The sooner she moved on—went back to whatever upscale neighborhood she'd come from—the better. "Look, Sam." She tilted her head over the nickname, sliding thick chocolate hair over one shoulder. "You can't just tell a man you drew him as an evil gladiator villain and not cough up the goods."

Duke swallowed when a light came on in her eyes, a corner of her mouth ticking up.

"Why not?"

"Because it sounds badass." Duke realized he was massaging his right knee—the old injury tended to act up when he sat too long. "Most men would have a hard time being offended by someone drawing them that way."

"Yeah," she said, perking up in seeming agreement. "Probably, right?"

Duke shook his head. "Was that a question, or—"

"No, an answer." She waved a hand, before returning it to the book. "Have you heard the story of David and Goliath?"

"You have been sent here to confuse me, Sam."

She laughed, a textured, throaty sound. "Why did you immediately start calling me Sam? You didn't even take a warm-up lap with Samantha."

"This isn't a three syllable establishment."

"Oh? I missed the sign on the way in." She stared at him a moment, as if he'd grown another foot, before visibly shaking herself. "Back to David and Goliath."

"I know it. Underdog story. Slingshot."

Her breath rushed out. "Thanks, Cliff."

Duke lifted his eyebrows. "Who?"

"Cliff Notes," Sam mumbled. "Never mind."

Amusement wafted in his chest, moving higher, higher, until Duke was fighting a smile. "That's not bad."

"What?"

"You calling me Cliff Notes." When she went back to staring at him, Duke shifted in his chair. Mostly because Sam staring at him gave him permission to stare back and that would only lead to trouble. Women were not on his agenda, let alone this drop-dead gorgeous out of towner so far out of his league it wasn't even funny. "So, uh…I'm Goliath in this drawing."

She tugged the book away from her body, gaze running over what Duke assumed was the sketch. "I'm not sure you should be anymore." Above her head, the sound of a baseball cracking off wood sounded, but Duke didn't look up. "It's important I get the characterization right. Can I get a do over?"

Huh. He kind of wanted to see the evil gladiator, but didn't much appreciate the idea of her feeling disappointed in herself. "What are you going to draw me as this time?"

"A grizzled sea captain."

Christ, this woman was a trip and a half. "Have at it."

A flush of relief coasted over her features, making Duke's pulse stutter…and keep on stuttering. As her pencil scratched over the fresh sheet of paper, she didn't seem to notice a dozen people discreetly moving behind her to watch the show. She must have been good, too, because heads bobbed, elbows nudged. Wasn't every day Hook residents were impressed by something, so by the time she finished, Duke could admit to a touch of impatience to see the results. Especially considering he wouldn't have pegged himself as a sea captain in a million years.

Finally she took a deep breath and turned the notebook around. Before he could stop it, a slow whistle passed beneath his breath. The drawing wasn't simply *good*; it belonged in a museum or something. The level of detail she'd managed to include in such a short time…it blew his fucking mind. His chest had been drawn large, decorated with embroidery and rows of shaded buttons, the hat sitting low over Pencil Duke's eyes, but not enough to hide his "you talkin' to me?" expression.

"I gave you a sword," she murmured, watching him carefully. "Since you didn't get to see yourself as an evil gladiator."

Duke leaned in to get a better look, clearing his throat to disguise the stool's groaning protest. "That's one mean looking sword—" He cut himself off when his gaze finally reached his caricature's lower half. A peg leg. She'd drawn him with a peg leg. Duke searched her face for some trace of teasing but found none. Didn't stop an annoying weight of discomfort from settling in his chest. For some reason, he didn't like this woman knowing he had a weakness. "It's good, Sam. Real good," Duke finished, sitting back in his stool and trying—failing—to focus on baseball.

He could feel her watching, could sense her confusion. What was wrong with him? Making this sweetheart feel poorly over noticing his injury, pointing it out. That wasn't right. Duke reached out to set his empty bottle on the bar, intending to give the drawing a closer look, the attention it deserved. But he paused when Sam flipped the notebook page over, ripping it out...and setting the gladiator drawing on his lap.

Another incredible sketch, if slightly more hurried than the second one. But what caught Duke's attention was the gladiator's leg. It had a deep wound, blood gushing down around the leather-wrapped ankle. But that made no sense. She'd drawn the sketch before he'd walked across the bar. "How did you know about my limp when you drew this?"

Samantha frowned. "You have a limp?"

"Yeah." Why couldn't he fill his lungs properly? "Got hit with some shrapnel while I was stationed overseas. With the

Army."

"Oh. I'm...sorry." She split a look between him and the notebook, still held to her chest. "It must have been the way you were leaning on the bar. Does it bother you?"

"Does it bother *you*?"

"No," she whispered, her knees pressing tight. "No, it makes you even more resilient."

Duke was still trying to decide on a reaction to that unexpected answer when Samantha started...packing up? She replaced the notebook in her bag and took out a purple wallet. Then she extricated a ten-dollar bill and wedged it beneath her martini glass. With a shrug, she picked up the drink, drained it, and set it back down on the money.

"Where are you going?" Duke shouted before pulling back on his reins to lower his voice. "You can't just draw me as a sea captain and leave."

Samantha slid off her stool, dragging the dress up two sweet thighs that matched her two sweet tits. "Telling me what I can't do? You're being presumptuous again, Duke."

There were a handful of certainties in Duke's life. One, baseball. Two, his tools. Grease. Working with his hands. Three, barbequing on summer Saturdays. Four, he didn't have any use for women, romantically speaking. Five, this wasn't going to be the last time he saw Sam.

She hitched her satchel up onto her right shoulder, dropping a hand to her belly to rub in a circle. "Can you point me toward the closest restaurant?"

"No. I can't."

Her mumbled response sounded something like *touchy, touchy*, but she moved for the door before he could ask for clarification. Duke followed her out into the night, ignoring the curious bar folk — his lifelong neighbors and coworkers — who watched them from the window. And no wonder, since he'd followed a woman from the bar exactly zero times before tonight. Hell, he usually never left his seat. "I can't direct you to the nearest restaurant because nothing is open in Hook past ten."

Nose wrinkling, she scanned the block. "There's no diner?" He shook his head. "What about a deli?" Another shake. "A bodega where I can get an egg sandwich?"

Duke pointed at her. "Manhattan girl."

"Guilty." A growl kicked up in the vicinity of her stomach. "And hungry."

Manhattan. Not far in terms of miles, but she might as well be on a different planet. "Wherever you're staying… there has to be something to eat there."

She didn't respond, but the way her shoulders sagged told Duke no, there wasn't. Jesus, he was actually going to feed this woman, wasn't he? Yeah. No choice in the matter. He was good and stuck. For the next hour, anyway. Once he dropped her off, that would be it. No numbers exchanged. Nothing. "Come on, Sam. I know a place not too far away." He gestured with a sweep of his arm. "My truck is this way. Try not to chew on the seats."

Chapter Two

Duke had reverted back to evil gladiator, it seemed. Back inside The Third Shift, he'd softened into weathered sea captain, but as they stalked toward his truck, his limp getting less noticeable the closer they got, she could picture the leather battle gear climbing up his back and slithering around his calves. And it seemed his reformation was luring her back in time as well, because she sorely wanted to pick up a stone and hurl it at his flexing, mile-wide back.

This wasn't what Samantha had in mind when she'd ventured into The Third Shift. People doing favors for others led to being grateful. Or doing favors in return. *Owing* someone. She only owed one person in this world—Renner—and even he, the one person she trusted in the world, had found a way to use that trust for his own personal gain. That wouldn't be the case with Duke, though, right? She lived a world away in Manhattan and, after tonight, they would be back to being strangers.

"I didn't ask you to take me out for food," she mumbled, trotting to keep up with his long strides. "I have a protein bar in my bag that'll hold me over until tomorrow—"

"I know a place that makes the best egg sandwiches you'll ever eat," Duke said without turning around.

Being somewhat of an egg sandwich connoisseur, Samantha had to admit that bold statement piqued her interest. "What makes them the best?"

"The taste."

Samantha turned on a heel and walked in the opposite direction. But she'd only made it about three steps when Goliath took her hand. And she gasped at the feel—actually gasped—ogling his appendage like it were made of thorns. Which wasn't far off. His palms and fingertips were blunt and rough. As though someone had taken sandpaper to them and rubbed vigorously, leaving scars to cover the damage. His hand was warm eroded stone. Why did it feel so wonderful?

Usually, she avoided gestures such as holding hands like the plague. They were a gateway drug to more elaborate expressions of affection. Such as tender cheek cradling, day trips to Vermont to see the fall leaves. Or wedding engagements.

Shivering, Samantha cast the thought aside. Been there, done that.

She moved her gaze higher, higher, until her neck was craned enough to meet Duke's eyes, which weren't quite narrowed enough to hide the fact that she'd startled him. By walking away or gasping like a loser? Hard to tell.

"The egg sandwiches aren't on the menu at this bakery. But the guy makes them in back for regulars after hours." Duke's thumb slid over Samantha's palm—just a tiny centimeter—before he dropped her hand as if it were on fire. "He makes sausage rolls, too, but I wouldn't recommend them unless your stomach is made of iron."

"Did you hear about the guy who got a job at the bakery?"

Duke shifted. "No."

Why am I doing this to myself? "He kneaded the dough."

Behind them, the bar door creaked up and slammed, the sound of baseball growing louder, then quiet. It reminded Samantha of the *badump-bum* drum roll that used to be delivered in old comedy clubs after a punch line. So, of course, she started to laugh, her fingers lifting and pressing against her lips in an attempt to keep a lid on the sound. No dice. There she was, laughing like a loon on a dark street, with Goliath staring her down. No wonder she usually stayed locked inside her office.

"I'm not going to stop making the bad jokes. I've tried." She sighed, kind of wishing they were still holding hands just so she could memorize the sensation. "So if you only like good jokes, this might be the end of the line for us."

He was quiet way too long. "Who said it was a bad joke?"

"Your lack of reaction."

"I've got too many things that require reactions right now."

Maybe it was silly—or a product of her lack of social activity—but she found that confusing statement rather comforting. "So this isn't the end of the line?"

Another pause that lasted far longer than she liked. "Not yet."

But it *would* end. She read that confirmation between the lines and it eased her somewhat. "When will that be—"

"Let's go." He strode off, back in the direction of his truck, leaving Samantha frowning after him. Best egg sandwich, huh? She'd see about that. Visualizing a giant puddle of mud for Duke to step in, a smile replaced her frown and she jogged after him. When they reached his oversized pickup, she was surprised to find it clean as a whistle, the surface glinting beneath the flickering streetlight.

She paused at the back bumper, removing the cell phone from her purse and snapping a picture of the license plate, her fingers flying over the screen to open a series of apps, accessing her camera roll—

"What are you doing?"

"I'm scheduling a tweet on TweetDeck. Of your license plate." She replaced the phone in her bag. "If I'm not home safe in an hour, your license plate gets tweeted along with the word *help*. In all caps."

"TweetDeck."

He'd never uttered the word before—that much was obvious. And it played right into his ancient gladiator persona so much, Samantha smiled.

It stayed in place as he rounded back from the driver's side, propping an elbow on the open truck cab, the vehicle dipping under his weight. "So this tweet thing...it's like insurance? It would let everyone know you're in trouble?"

"Yes." Maybe threatening someone via social media wasn't the norm. Her smile slipped away at the thought. "It's nothing personal, it just seemed like the most efficient way to not get killed. You know, on short notice."

"No, it's good." He dug out his own phone—a model Samantha was sure had been put out to pasture years ago—blunt fingers hunting and pecking their way over the surface. "Say the name again. I'm texting it to my sisters."

Oh. Ah. "To keep them safe?"

He gave an absent nod, totally unaware that his gladiator armor had slunk to the ground, replaced by a waving patriotic super hero cape.

"Um. TweetDeck."

"How the fuck do they name these things?" he muttered, still jabbing the screen. "What are they doing to us? Everything sounds ridiculous now."

"Who are *they*?"

"That's what I'd like to know." Apparently finished with his mission to protect, Duke shoved the cell back into his pocket and made for the driver's side once more. "Hop in, Sam. *Tweet*Deck is keeping you safe," he said wryly.

She hesitated for only a beat before joining Duke in the truck. Or rather, clumsily plopping on the vinyl seat after heaving herself into the monster-sized vehicle. "How many sisters do you have?"

His sigh could have blown a ship out to sea. "Four."

Wow. Five kids. Having been an only child half her life, Samantha could only marvel at the idea. "Are you on a five-way text with them?"

"Yes. Biggest mistake of my life." He pulled out onto the dark street, hitting the blinker and turning right. "It's like the mafia, these group texts. Once you're in, you're in for life."

Another laugh slipped out. Samantha stared out at the road, kind of thrown by the whole situation, while being somewhat proud she'd gotten herself into it. Her Friday nights were usually spent in the park, sketching passersby or watching Bob Ross reruns on YouTube. Instead, she was in a pickup truck, being taken out for a meal by a big, impressive man. His casual attitude assured her this interaction would end on a tidy note afterward, no muss no fuss. *Not bad, ol' Sam.*

"So, Manhattan girl, what brought you to Hook? The scenery?"

Samantha had to admit the place could use some sprucing, but there was an air of charm to the houses they passed. Pride went into maintaining them, if not money or extensive landscaping. But it was the kind of town kids could leave their bikes on the lawn overnight, which was more than she could say for Manhattan. "I'm…meeting with my brother on Monday. He's out of town until then, so I'm staying in his place." She could feel Duke's attention on her profile. "And I guess I just wanted to see something other than my own four walls."

Duke grunted. "I assume you're an illustrator."

"Yes," she answered, warmth moving in her breast. But the warmth dissipated when she remembered the dream business she'd been *this close* to starting was no longer a reality. *No, you'll get there. It'll just take longer now.* "I illustrate children's books." A sudden thought had her head whipping around. "You don't have kids, do you?"

"Jesus, no." He rolled his neck. "But I do have a Marcy." The cantaloupe-sized muscles of his biceps shifted as he took another turn. "My friends have a four-year-old and they all live in my guest house." When he visibly softened, Samantha battled the urge to unbuckle her seat belt and smack kisses all over his unshaved cheeks. "I give her the non-organic juice boxes, she let's me watch SportsCenter. We get each other."

What if she just threw her arms out the open window and sobbed on behalf of all womankind? If they knew about this guy in Manhattan, the next bus to Hook would be standing room only. Instead, he'd gotten her. The one who'd pass the bus, sprinting in the opposite direction. "You babysit Marcy?"

Another grunt. "What about you, Sam? Kids?" His big shoulders tensed. "Husband?"

"No," she said quietly. Working on children's books put her in contact with all things kid-related, and truthfully, she adored youngsters. Their enthusiasm and lack of verbal filter. The business she'd designed—but might never see daylight— would have put her in contact with kids on a daily basis. And she'd looked forward to that. Making sure they knew their best effort was fantastic, instead of always pointing out what they could have done better. She knew too well what the quest for approval from a parent felt like—and giving her admiration and support freely? She wanted that with her whole heart, even if having her own children would never be a reality. "What about you, Duke?" She cleared the scratchiness from her throat. "Do you work in town?" *What makes your hands so full of character?*

"I'm a machinery mechanic at the factory." As if he'd timed it, they passed by the newly redesigned Bastion Enterprises, the harshness of its waist-high cinderblock walls made more accessible by greenery. Her eco-conscious brother's idea, if she remembered correctly. And this was where Samantha told Duke her brother owned the factory where he worked. That he was—essentially—driving around the boss's little sister. But as the giant structure slipped past in the driver's side window, Samantha remained quiet.

• • •

Samantha was, quite obviously, Renner Bastion's little sister.

Everyone had their calendars marked for Monday, when the boss man was due to plague everyone's work station. That was when Samantha claimed she would meet with her brother. Two people who didn't belong in Hook, being there at the same time? Yeah. Not a coincidence.

Duke waited for her to inform him of the relation, feeling a stab of disappointment when she stayed silent. A ridiculous way to feel, when he understood her reason. Everyone in town worked for Renner Bastion and there was no love lost between the uptight, citified asshole and Hook's population. But frankly, no one gave a good goddamn, so long as they got paid on Friday. Bastion showed up once a month and ruffled everyone's feathers before flying off to oversee his other interests. It was a bearable arrangement, so everyone kept their heads down and worked, same as they always did. And if once in a while, someone grudgingly admitted the working conditions had vastly improved since Bastion taking the helm? They were all in agreement it only slightly discounted his asshole status.

Duke had been born and raised within Hook's borders.

Not only did he know every name and face, but he knew their drink of choice, how they preferred a burger cooked, and their work ethic. In order to miss Samantha's presence in Hook for his entire thirty-two years, he would've had to be blind and deaf. And still…he would've caught her brandied plum scent. So even then, he'd have known.

He knew she was around now. Ah hell, did he ever. The seat of his truck damn near swallowed her petite form right up, which led to bad thoughts. *Hungry* ones. Like how easily he could toss her up against a wall and keep her there. Wouldn't even need the use of his hands, at least not for anything but… feeling. Smoothing up and down her ass. Feeling her legs go limp when he finished her off once, then started again. If she thought she'd been sweaty walking into The Third Shift, she hadn't seen nothing. He'd take her until she left an imprint on the wall.

Christ. He needed to pull himself together. She was Bastion's sister.

And while he was on the subject of "things he couldn't do"? Bringing a woman home was at the top of his list. Not only did his living situation leave something to be desired—as in peace and fucking quiet—he wasn't looking for a woman. He had four broken-hearted sisters living in his house, each with their own personal ex-husband voodoo doll, and if Duke knew one thing, it was that he wasn't any better than those ex-husbands. He wanted three things out of life: sleep, sports, and steak. He might have given each of those poor saps a sound beating—they'd hurt his sisters, after all—but damn if he could have done any better with his own woman.

He wouldn't be finding out for sure any time soon.

Duke was distracted from his thoughts when Samantha crossed her legs on the seat—giving him a tempting eyeful of inner thigh—and pulled out her notebook. "Can you tell me about your sisters?" she asked, pencil poised over the blank white space. "Start with the oldest."

Despite his usual irritation with the four tornados that continually wreaked havoc on his life, his lips twitched. "We've got four L's. Luanne is the oldest. Then along came Lorraine and Lisa—they're twins. And rounded out with Lacey."

"Your parents didn't include you in the L theme?"

"My mother didn't think of it until after I was already here. But sometimes my sisters call me Luke, instead of Duke." He squinted through the windshield, relieved the light was on at their destination. "They think they're funny."

"*I* think they're funny."

"Sure you do. You're the keeper of bad jokes."

When she kind of breathe-giggled, Duke's stomach tied up in a knot. Of course she had to be a little sweetheart. Of course she had to laugh at herself. "Hey, I even had my own one-woman show." She shrugged. "Really, it was just a play on words."

Duke fought a grin in the wake of the pun. It was official. She was the polar opposite of her brother. And that couldn't have been worse news for him. He needed to fill up her stomach with food, drop her off, and get on his not-so-merry way. "You're hilarious. Let's go."

He waited at the curb as she climbed out of his truck, kind of the way someone descends a small skyscraper. His hands itched to ease her down, body poised to lunge if she slipped, but no way would he help. *Hands off.* Not only was she a woman, which was enough reason to keep his distance, but overstepping his bounds could lead to the axe at work. Not an option when he was feeding four sisters. Plus housing his best friend, Vaughn, Vaughn's wife, River, and their daughter, Marcy, in the small guest house above his garage.

"You didn't finish telling me about your sisters," Samantha said, notebook tucked beneath her arm, as she fell into step with him. "How about this? Describe each of them in one word and I'll draw based on that."

"Do you have to draw everyone you meet?"

Her forehead wrinkled. "Sometimes I don't see anything when I meet a person. That's usually a bad sign." She smiled at him. "I've seen three things for you already."

"Lucky me."

"I know," she said brightly.

He stopped outside the bakery and rapped on the door. "What was the third?"

She moved her hair around a bunch, like she was trying to confuse him into forgetting he'd asked the question. "Okay, start with Luanne. One word."

Avoiding, huh? Maybe she'd seen him as a garbage man. Or a porn star. "Luanne? Eh…Real Housewives."

"That's two words."

Duke lifted a shoulder. "That's what I got." Guilt kicked him in the gut. "Also…generous. She's generous."

Thank God the bakery owner took that moment to unlock and answer the door, greeting Duke with a fist bump. "Okay," the man said. "What we got here? Someone's hungry or what?"

Samantha drifted closer to Duke's side and *God*, it took every ounce of willpower not to drape an arm over her shoulders, tug her close. Take a big sniff of her hair and claim her in some small way. She looked like an overachiever honor student standing there, ready to be introduced so she could begin speaking. Someone needed to remind her she was in New Jersey, where women spoke however and whenever they damn well felt like it. "Hey, Buddy. This is Sam. She's on the hunt for an egg sandwich."

As Duke predicted she would, Samantha juggled her notepad, holding out her hand to the middle-aged man for a shake. "Nice to meet you. I'm sorry it's so late."

Buddy might as well have had hearts flashing in his eyes. "S'no problem, honey. Come in, come in."

They followed the owner inside, taking a table he

indicated near the window. Then Duke and Samantha were back to being alone, Buddy having waltzed back into the kitchen. When Samantha folded her hands on her notepad and watched him expectantly, Duke blew out a breath. "Lorraine in one word? You could say she's thoughtful. Brings our older neighbors dinner when they're not feeling up to cooking. Lisa is organized. Gets everyone where they're going. Lacey… she's the baby. Always crying. So…heart, I guess. Heart."

Samantha's chin had come to rest on her hand, but it slipped off now, dropping her head into a catching bob. The kind people did when they fell asleep in the car. "You seem to know them very well."

Duke almost omitted the reality of his living situation—the way any man might try to make his lifestyle appear ideal to a beautiful woman—but no way could he let himself skate. That would signal an effort to keep one particular woman around and, yeah, not happening. Honestly, he'd be doing her a favor by making himself *even less* appealing. "I have no choice but to know my sisters well. They all live with me."

Her mouth fell open. "All four of them?"

"That's right." Duke drummed his fingers on the table. "Made sure they were all married before I enlisted in the Army. Came back two years later and they were all divorced, living in my house."

Those big doe eyes fell to her sketch pad, as if she could see all four tragedies playing out on its surface in vivid color. "That's awful. It's awful when commitments are broken. No matter who's at fault, people get hurt." She went a little lifeless in her chair, laying her pencil down and falling back.

Oh man, Duke didn't like that. Didn't like Samantha anything but animated and inquisitive and making bad jokes that were actually kind of great. "What's wrong with you?"

His booming question made her whole body jerk upright. "I was just thinking that people break promises so easily.

Don't they? And I'm no better. I've done it, too."

"If you broke a promise, sweetheart, I'm sure there was a damn good reason." Duke might have met her that very night, but he would've staked his life savings on that certainty. And yeah, that certainty scared the hell out of him, but there it was. Not budging, either. "Who did you break a promise to?"

When Buddy split the moment in half by setting a plate of egg sandwiches down on the table and clapping his hands, Duke ignored the surge of frustration. *Come on, man, you got off lucky.* The less he knew about this city girl, the easier it would be when he dropped her off. Duke checked his watch without really seeing the time, before nabbing an egg-stuffed biscuit off the plate. He'd already devoured half his sandwich before Samantha even took a bite.

"What are you waiting for?"

"Is this a date?"

"No," Duke rumbled. "You need to know that before eating?"

"Yes, because I, um…just realized I spent the last of my cash at the bar." The hand holding her biscuit lowered, even as she eyed it ravenously. "And if this isn't a date, I have to at least pay my half, right?"

Duke tossed the last bite into his mouth, wondering how often she dated. Not frequently, he was guessing, based on her needing the situation clarified. How did this girl walk one block without someone begging to buy her dinner? "I've got you covered."

"So, *not* a date." She looked a little too relieved for his liking. "Thank you."

Her eyelids fluttered down on the first bite, a long, drawn-out hum making Duke's mouth go dry. He tore his attention off Samantha's visible pleasure only to raise a *what-the-fuck* eyebrow at a rapt Buddy—who pivoted back toward the kitchen—then went straight back to watching her. *Goddamn,* she was something, turning chewing into an art form. Even her pinkie stuck out. If that didn't reiterate their obvious mismatch, nothing would.

"You were right," she said, finally, taking a napkin from the dispenser to dab at her mouth. "It's the best egg sandwich I've ever had. I have to Yelp this."

"What now?"

"Nothing."

There was a needle in Duke's side, prodding him, dying to know about this promise she'd broken. Hell, that was only a single item on the list of questions banging around like slap shots in his head. But he refrained, settling for watching her eat instead. Which he liked just a touch too much. Liked knowing his money would be the reason she went to bed with a full stomach. He could envision her in panties and no bra, stretching out, yawning with sleepy, sated satisfaction, remembering Duke had put sustenance in her belly. Eager to thank him, but...he'd be long gone, wouldn't he?

Damn, he was starting to sweat and it had nothing to do with the heat wave. Droplets trickled down his stomach, his lower back. The way her mouth looked, chewing...

With a couple bites to go, she offered him the rest, but Duke declined, dropping the appropriate amount of bills on the table then rising, careful to keep his T-shirt pulled down over his lap. Because holy fuck, his cock was at full mast for sweet Samantha. Getting her home and walking away wouldn't be easy, but he'd do it. He'd lived through a tour overseas and over a decade of factory work. Leaving this girl untouched on her doorstep should be a walk in the park.

Uh-huh.

After calling good-byes to Buddy, they got back in the truck and turned back the direction they'd come. "Where are you staying?"

He already knew. *Everyone* knew Bastion had the

apartment above the stationary shop. It was one of the only rentals in town. The factory workers had surmised he used it for tax purposes—possibly getting a break for being a New Jersey resident and business owner—but he did stay there at least one night per month, when he came to poke his nose into factory operations.

"I'm at…" Samantha dug through her bag and took out her phone. She rattled off the address twice and Duke nodded once. "Thank you for doing this. You didn't have to."

"Don't mention it."

They were almost to the apartment when Samantha sighed—loudly. And then she did it again, running her palms down her knees, back up. "Duke, I have to tell you something."

Here it comes. He fought to keep his smile hidden. "No, you don't."

"Yes." She waited until he pulled up alongside the curb, gathering her bag close and leveling him with a solemn look. "This is my brother's—*step*brother, actually…this is his apartment. His name is Renner Bastion and he owns the factory. Where you work." She pushed open the door and dangled one leg out. "I doubt I'll ever see you again. And if you found out, I didn't want you to remember me as a liar. Even by omission."

Panic started to rise in Duke's throat when she jumped out of the car, teetering adorably on one leg when she landed. *Uh-oh. Oh, Christ.* He *really* didn't like her going away. "Sam—"

"It was a superhero. The third drawing idea I had for you." She closed the passenger door, waving and calling through the window. "Good-bye, Duke."

Good-bye not good night. The finality of that word was what fucked him, made his insides seize. She'd barely made it inside the vestibule before Duke was rounding the truck's front bumper, going after her.

What are you doing?

Chapter Three

Even through the glass vestibule door, the booted footsteps that followed Samantha were unmistakable. She could all but feel the ground shake. And then her whole body decided to join the party, nerves jangling like a change purse, knees trembling with a fight or flight instinct. Had she forgotten something in the car...or was this it? Was Duke going to kiss her? Somewhere around the first stop light on the way home, she'd allowed herself to ponder the possibility. What would it feel like, having that bristly jaw scraping her cheeks? What would a man with so much obvious life experience kiss like? And...oh, the big one...where would his Goliath-sized hands go?

All that wishful thinking had been premature. For one, it hadn't even been a date. He'd said so himself—*vehemently*, even. Two, he couldn't have communicated his lack of interest more clearly if he'd been wearing a blinking "no thank you" necklace. Duke was a provider, pure and simple. And much as it irked her independent spirit, she'd been ripe for saving. Girl enters bar, stomach growls, big hero saves the day. She'd been pretty cool with the concept because his negative response to dating appeared to match hers, keeping the whole interaction safe. Not a string in sight. Now…she wasn't so sure.

Be cool. Be cool. Samantha turned around just as Duke pushed into the small vestibule, instantly making the room feel like a doll house. "Hi again," she breathed, because oh my God, this man was such a…man. Just a huge, rough and gruff, hot without being handsome *man*. They didn't grow them in Manhattan like this. Square footage was at such a premium, Duke would pay through the nose for enough space to stretch out. And why was she thinking about real estate? "What did I drop?"

He propped a hand on the wall to his right—reminding her of a mighty tree branch—and leaned. *His leg hurts.* She knew that somehow, knew he was sensitive about the apparent injury, so she focused on not looking down. Pretty easy, considering the fascinating quality of his face. The indecision written on his weathered features. "Where's your phone?"

"My phone." Recognition was an ice-cold blast in the face. "Oh, you want to make sure I un-schedule the murder tweet."

Crinkles formed at the corners of his eyes. "Your what?"

"Never mind." Dying a little inside, Samantha pulled out her phone, intending to open the app in question. The one preparing to send out her murder tweet—which wasn't even a *thing*—

Duke pinched the phone between his index finger and thumb, lifting it away, the way a giant might pluck a car off the road. "I'm not worried about the tweet, because I'm leaving you safe at your door, aren't I? Someone asks me about you, that's what I'll tell them, because it's true. And it would be true, sweetheart, *any* time you were in my company. Every time." He held her attention until she nodded. "I'm giving you my number, in case you run into a problem. Like a broken air conditioner—or a broken ankle—while you're in Hook."

Truth be told, it took a moment for alarm to taper in, because she was busy picturing Duke in a shiny red cape, the material snapping in the imaginary breeze. But the words phone number penetrated without delay. "Right. Broken stuff." She tried to get a read on his intentions and failed. "Those are the *only* reasons I should call you."

His nod came after a small hesitation, but it was firm. "If I were the dating type…" He cleared his throat, shifting on his injured leg with a barely-there wince. "But I'm not. Since we're being truthful with each other, Sam, I'd rather swim in shark infested waters than date, and I doubt there would be much difference between the two activities."

"I see." Oh, now *this* was an absolute riot. They were *both* anti-relationship? Somehow she'd traveled forty miles and run smack into her male counterpart without realizing. Here she'd thought it was only her in which he'd lacked interest, but it was women in general. "You're sure it has nothing to do with my brother?"

A muscle in his cheek jumped. "I'm not real fond of the suggestion another man would keep me from you. So, no. I don't give a shit if you're related." He visibly calmed himself. "That's if I were the dating type—"

"I don't need your number, Duke," Samantha interrupted, hoping to put him at ease. Attempting to explain what it was like to be content alone? Yeah, she knew how difficult it could be. She couldn't, however, account for the ridiculous little stab of hurt at knowing she fell into the same category as everyone else. "Look. I've lived on my own for seven years. If I break my ankle, I'll call an ambulance. If the air conditioner goes out, I'll call a repairman. These are little tricks one learns when they have an IQ higher than a donkey."

His mouth leaped up at one end, but instead of laughing outright, he held up her phone. "What's the password?"

She reached for the phone, but he only held it aloft. Which basically put it at the height of a two-story building. "Not cool. I'm only going to delete your number once I'm inside."

"Password."

Samantha took a deep breath to center herself. "One one one one."

Duke shook his head. "Jesus. I hope you aren't storing the nuclear codes in here."

Her resulting burst of laughter took her by surprise, giving Samantha no hope of containing it. She was surprised the vestibule's window didn't shatter under the impact. "Not bad," she sniffed.

Now that they were in the light, she could see his eyes were a mixture of blue and hazel, and that unique gaze pinned her beneath it now, flipping a pancake-sized object in her stomach. He stepped closer, just one step, and it set her pulse off like a roaring crowd. Was he going to kiss her? A *shark*? Just when she was positive it would happen, that he would stoop down and lay one on her, Duke stopped. With only a miniscule separation between them, he keyed in his number and pressed save. "Are you going to stay put here until your brother comes back, or what?"

Samantha would have laughed if Duke wasn't looming over her, emitting enough masculinity to cast an entire action flick. Renner wasn't returning until Monday. Even she couldn't perform a solo "Netflix and chill" that long. "Um...no?"

With his lips parted, she could see his tongue push into his cheek. "What are you planning?"

"I haven't decided yet," she whispered, as if imparting a grave secret. "But this building looks about the right height for base jumping."

A low rumble kicked up, courtesy of Duke. "Not bad."

There was no helping the smile. She could feel it transforming her expression like a defiant weed that continued to grow back. Around Duke. And as he watched it germinate, his own lips parted, his big body performing a kind of heaving breath, a step closer—*do it do it kiss me this is insane*—but he paused, handing her the cell phone. "Just…call me if you need something, Sam."

She was still nodding as Duke exited the vestibule, his gait stilted by the limp, big shoulders bunched in the fading light, muscles playing on the back of his T-shirt in a hypnotic taunt. And then…then Samantha lifted up her phone and dialed the most recent saved number, sighing when she saw Duke had entered himself as *E. Vil Gladiator.*

What am I doing?

Maybe the major life decision she'd made this week had loosened a little ball of rebellion that continued to roll through her veins. Or perhaps knowing Duke didn't want anything serious made dialing the number acceptable. Safe. Her personal life had played second fiddle to her career so long, she hadn't stopped to consider the possibility of having both, without having to commit full-time to the former. She wanted a kiss from this man. It could be the physical symbol of becoming her own person again. The fact that he wanted nothing beyond this drop-off could be perfect. Definitely not disappointing.

The time for doubt faded when Duke halted on the sidewalk, just before the street, tugging the phone from his jeans pocket. Samantha watched, breath racing in and out, as he squinted at the ancient green screen. The device fell to his outer thigh, his head falling forward, before he lifted and answered. "Yeah."

"I need something."

A low, shaking curse. "*Sam.*"

God, the way his voice deepened on that single word made her blood flame. "Yes." *No guts, no glory.* "I-I could use a good night kiss."

His stroll back toward the door seemed to take an hour. "You could use it?" He stopped, arms braced on the building's doorframe, his breath fogging up the glass. "Or you need it?"

For the first time in…maybe forever, Samantha's loins started to ache, due to something other than her own imagination. And damn it all, even her crazy imagination couldn't have conjured up a Duke. His blunt chin, the scratchy-looking hair on his belly. "I need it."

The condensation left by his breaths appeared faster, undeniable proof he was affected, too, despite his desire to stay free of entanglements. Just like her. "One kiss. I can't give you any more than that." His fist came up to bang against the glass. "Don't ask me to bring you inside. Please. I'm not the kind of man you're looking for. But you'd get me, regardless, if we fucked. You hearing me, sweetheart?"

Samantha's vocal cords had lost the ability to function, so she simply hung up the phone, stowed it, and set the bag in the vestibule's corner. And waited, palms raking up and down the skirt of her dress. Duke watched her through the door a beat, before jerking it open. There was no slow motion coming together or easing into the kiss, either. No, Duke…stormed Samantha. And…and he was out of practice. She could tell right away. He couldn't seem to stop baring his teeth long enough to kiss her properly, his hands settling on her hips and gripping way too tight. Bruises. She'd have bruises and they hadn't even begun yet. Everything about the hovering—the brink, his harsh, growling hesitation—turned Samantha on. This was unusual for him…he didn't *do* this.

All pent up. The giant's adrenaline was all *pent up*.

"You look so…" He shuddered, lifting her off the floor so he could suck the skin of her neck, his arm like steel around her lower back. "You look so fucking sexy in that dress, I—"

"Thank you," she whimpered, feet swinging, searching for purchase. The need for solid ground was gone a second later, however, when a thick, flexing thigh shoved in between her legs, pressing against her juncture with such unexpectedness, she tightened her limbs around it, gasping. "*Duke.*"

"We still being honest with each other, sweetheart?" He didn't wait for an answer, roughly gliding his hands down, hooking them beneath her knees and sliding her higher on his thigh. The move dragged her core over so many ridges of sinew, she lost count, a moan slipping free. "Someday, when you're long gone and you've forgotten my name, I'll still be wondering what you'd have felt like. Taking me. Working me up, letting me take you down. *Hold* you down."

The images his words projected might have alarmed her, coming from someone else. But…not *this* man. She could feel his restraint, feel his pulsing beneath the power he wore like a second skin. "Is that what you like?" Samantha whispered. "You like—"

"*Don't.*" Duke's mouth began to feast. There was simply no other description. His tongue catching her unaware long enough to slip inside, making a bold, groaning claim on hers. Had—*whoa*—had she actually thought him out of practice? Clearly she'd jumped the gun. Or Duke just caught back on *quick*. Because Samantha lost actual time, reality flickering to a fuzzy, black-edged dreamscape. And when she regained focus, she was rocking up and back on his thigh, hands fisted in the shirt covering his shoulders. Climbing, seeking, desperate to sink deeper into the kiss.

Duke bent her back over his forearm, treating her mouth to conduct void of gentleness, unless she counted the strained effort she could sense him making to stay at some level of decent. Respectful. Which was almost comical, considering she was attempting to drive herself to climax with his tree trunk thigh. But God, she couldn't stop, *could not stop*. He was abundant, ravenous male and all that energy was alive for *her*. Even his smell was perfect in its rawness. Sweat and beer and aftershave. God, yes. Refusing to waste this chance to feel—feel so much after experiencing nothing for too long—she kicked off a sandal and hooked a toe in Duke's belt loop, levering her body higher, giving herself a different angle to work his flexed leg. All the while his slanted mouth bore down, wet and rhythmic. No finesse involved, just natural male hunger.

When Samantha managed to scale him enough to feel his arousal against her hip, she once again teetered on the edge of fantasy and reality, breaking away with a sound full of aching. "Oh...oh my God."

"Yeah? How do you think I feel?" His hands were shaking fists in the hem of her dress. "Cute little thing can't keep her pussy off me. Can't stop sucking my tongue so hard I feel it down in my balls." His voice was nothing but a scarred rasp, a red flush decorating his rugged cheekbones. "Haven't been at this in a while, but I know this isn't how a first kiss goes. With a woman trying to get fucked standing up."

"*First* kiss?"

"*Only*." He licked his lips after growling the word, gaze fastened on her mouth, his erection heavy at her hip. "A man doesn't take a woman like you to bed and walk away. I can't afford to—"

"Get stuck. Trust me, I understand."

His nostrils flared on a heavy exhale. "Stuck? Wouldn't use that word. Not when I'm talking about you, Sam." Something seemed to occur to him then, his revved-up, tank-sized body stilling, before he walked them backward, levering Samantha against the door. The warmth of his breath pelted her lips, that thigh wedged so tight she felt dizzy. "If someone ever does hurt you like that...or treat you bad, you come *find* me. I'll..."

Butterflies went wild in her throat, set loose by the husky intensity of his tone, but a twinge of dread was mixed in, too. "You'll what?"

No longer was he looking at her, his brow furrowed as he stared at something that seemed far away. "I was going to say I'd make them sorry."

Big ol' born and bred hero. She'd never seen one up close before. Not of his caliber. "Why did you stop?"

Duke stepped back, allowing her feet to find the ground, body sliding down the door. Only an inch of space lay between them, but the withdrawal of actual touch made it feel like ten miles. And it was obvious they were both feeling the loss. Their hands lifted, fingers curling inward to prevent reaching, bodies shifting like they could pounce with the right cue. "I want to hurt them *now*," Duke grated. "Whether they treat you good or bad. *Fuck*, I just want to hurt them."

Heat walloped Samantha below the waist. This was what it felt like. To really be wanted, have another person call you *theirs* and mean it, whether she liked it or not. Whether *he* liked it or not. And Duke didn't like it. Maybe even resented her for instilling that possessiveness in him. Because he visibly snapped back into himself, regarding her like they hadn't just slayed each other with a kiss.

Stupid. The sense of betrayal that followed was so *stupid*. But it spread. And spread. Until her stomach felt lined with lead, dragging toward her knees. Without realizing it, had she opened herself up to this self-proclaimed unavailable man? Hadn't she dealt with enough disinterest in her lifetime? Whatever the reason, it was obvious pursuing the kiss had been a serious error in judgment.

One backward step put him at the door. "Look, I'm sorry. I shouldn't have come back in here." He dipped his chin, indicating the second entrance, clearly trying to be brisk, but unable to pull it off with his shoulders so tense. "You get inside and lock the door."

Samantha had already turned away before he finished speaking, rattling her keys into the lock. Perhaps it was the leftover adrenaline from the kiss or the possibility she would have made it happen even if he *were* the type of man who wanted a relationship. Whatever the reason, she couldn't get away from him fast enough. And his apology only made the bad decision sting worse. "Good-bye, Duke," she murmured.

The door closed on his hefty sigh.

Chapter Four

As soon as Duke set foot in the supermarket the next morning, he knew Samantha was inside. The checkout ladies—same ones had been there since he was in high school—were whispering to one another, craning their necks to get a good look down the aisles. And they had nothing on the stock boy who was texting so fast his fingers blurred. The kid's mouth was gaping open, as if he'd just seen a ghost or a Kardashian. Or, more likely, a white-hot beauty with a smile that could knock a man on his ass. Sure as shit, she'd knocked him straight onto his, which accounted for his piss-poor mood this morning.

Dammit, why couldn't she just stay put?

He'd been awake the whole goddamn night, a deadly mixture of guilty and horny. Unfortunately, the guilt over the well-concealed hurt he'd seen on Samantha's face overrode everything else, making him feel like the world's biggest asshole for wanting to jerk off. In the end, he'd laid there miserable, his cock feeling like a barbell on his stomach, wondering what the hell he could have done differently.

Women showed interest in him on occasion, but they were all Hook women. It was common knowledge Duke would just as soon wear a tiara than saddle up with a girlfriend, so they moved on to other pastures without him having to say a word. He'd tried to communicate his need to be alone to Samantha, but in the light of day, he could recall how thin the explanation had sounded, being spoken while looking into those rich doe eyes. He hadn't been convincing—not to himself nor Samantha—because their attraction had drowned him out.

What the hell had he been thinking, kissing her like that? Dragging her up his thigh and finding out how she tasted? The memory of those whimpers, the little scoot of her ass, would haunt him for years to come. Which was a fucking kicker considering his guilt prevented him from beating his meat.

Speaking of meat, customers were gravitating toward the rear of the market, giving Duke a clue where he would find Samantha. In the exact aisle he needed to pick up steaks for this afternoon's barbeque. That was if he were *looking* for Samantha, which he was not. Clearly, he couldn't control himself where the bad pun aficionado was concerned, so distance was now necessary to survival. Yes, survival. And if anyone found him clinging to bachelorhood amusing, Duke would simply direct them to his living room, where four sisters cried their hearts out on a daily basis over failed marriages, their bodies not being acceptable, men who didn't call after dates. The list went on.

Men were pricks, plain and simple. Himself included. His father had left his mother after she popped out their fifth child, moving on with so little fanfare Duke had spent years waiting for the fallout. But no, his father's move to North Carolina, his remarriage to a real estate agent, had been as seamless as popping open a beer. Their mother lived in Long Island now in a retirement village, happy enough to spend time with friends and receive visits from her children on occasion, but the bitterness Duke glimpsed when their father came up? The bitter sadness displayed by his sisters? He never, *ever*, wanted to put that on a woman's face. And he didn't know how he'd manage it. Only knew he would, probably without even trying.

Hell, look how easily he'd managed to disappoint Samantha last night by putting on the brakes. Truth was that's what happened in relationships. One person inevitably let down the other. And he had too much respect for women to make one miserable on his account. Never. Happening.

The image of Samantha's disappointed face wavered when her laughter rang out from the meat aisle, making Duke's abdominal muscles contract. *Laughter?* Apparently he was the *only* one who'd spent the night twisted in a knot. Knowing he shouldn't, but unable to contain his curiosity over what had made her laugh, Duke strode for the back of the market, red basket in hand. He needed steaks, after all. Didn't he? Saturday summer barbeques were a tradition he never broke, and he wouldn't start now over some city girl who couldn't stay put.

Duke stopped on a dime when Samantha came into view. Rather, Samantha, plus the three men surrounding her. *Christ.* Christ, his pulse kicked into high speed so fast lights winked in his vision. And his blood seemed heavier than usual, like maybe there was metal flowing in his veins, weighing him down. On top of everything, a burn had started in his ribcage. What was this? Was he having a fucking stroke?

No, but he was going to. If the motherfucker on the right moved even one inch closer to Samantha. Gorgeous, blushing Samantha in another dress, this one white, dotted with bright red flowers, making her look fresh and summery. Somewhere along the line, she must have been told her tits were one of her best features, because once again, they were pushed up in a way that was probably effortless, just ripe, dewy offerings that were covered enough to look innocently provocative. And they were way too close to three other sets of hands.

Duke knew the guys, same way he knew everyone in town. They ran the food truck that sat outside the factory, selling gyros and wrapped heroes out of a propped open window. They were on a first name basis with Duke, but he'd never taken the time to consider if they were…attractive to women. Were they?

Fuck if he knew. But he wasn't going to stand there and find out Samantha's opinion. The decision to interfere in the little back aisle rendezvous eased the burning in Duke's chest, but it was short lived, because of what happened next. She punned. And she punned hard. To someone that wasn't Duke.

"When the cannibal showed up late to lunch…" She paused for dramatic effect. "…they gave him the cold shoulder."

Of course, all three idiots doubled over laughing, slapping each other high-fives while Samantha watched in breathless surprise. Surprise over them laughing? Had Duke laughed at her jokes? He didn't think so. *See that? You* are *a prick.*

"Why couldn't you stay put, Sam?" Duke boomed, moving down the aisle, probably looking like some deranged serial killer and not giving a single care. "You, you, you." He jerked his chin toward the exit. "Hit the fucking bricks."

"What gives, Du—"

Duke silenced the brave man with a glare, who promptly joined the other two already slinking toward the door. He waited for them to vanish onto the street before facing Samantha, whose pretty face was the picture of disbelief. She lifted a finger and jabbed him hard in the shoulder. "*Presumptuous.*"

He moved past her, toward the waist-high refrigerator, shoveling steaks into his hand basket without even checking the quality. "Is this the plan you came up with for the weekend? Picking up men?"

"Worked with you," she returned. "Got a free egg sandwich and a ride home. Maybe I was just keeping my streak alive."

Duke ground his teeth together. "Finish your shopping. I'll walk you home."

"Oh…" She trailed off into a sputter. "*Please.* I think not."

He watched over his shoulder as she stormed down the aisle, ripping Oreos off the shelf and slamming them into her basket. An Entenmann's coffee cake followed. Then a bag of Cheetos. Duke turned on a heel and went after Samantha before the action even registered with his brain. "You can't exist on junk food. Put something real in there."

Samantha paused at a popcorn display, smiling at him as she lowered a blue and white box into her basket. "Mmmm. Butteriffic."

"Is this how you eat in Manhattan?"

"No." She continued on, turning right at the beverages aisle, loading the basket with Mountain Dew until Duke could see her arm was straining with the weight. So he reached out and tried to take it. And of course she held on, resulting in a tug of war right there in the aisle, as the checkout ladies pretended not to stare. "No, I don't usually eat like this. I'm usually really responsible with multi-grains and gluten frees and yogurt that's supposed to taste like key lime pie but really tastes like toothpaste."

God, she was right. That yogurt was a sin against humanity. "So you're doing this just to give me hives?"

"No again. Nothing I'm doing here. Is revolving. Around you. Duke." She hefted up her basket with a flourish. "I bid you good day."

"Wait." He stepped into Samantha's path, her flash of temper telling Duke he was lucky she had an armful or he'd be eating a right hook. "If you're usually so responsible, what…changed?"

"Nothing." Her demeanor shifted, going from irritated to resigned. "Everything." When the stock boy strolled by whistling, she lowered her voice. "I don't need to talk about it. I just need to buy this crappy food and that's my constitutional right. So, please move."

Damn it, she wasn't making this distance thing easy. *At all.* He wanted to wrap her up in a bear hug and whisper dumb, unmanly things in her ear. The way guys comforted women on television. The exact opposite way *he* comforted women. His technique involved a hearty pat on the back. Repairing something they hadn't realized was broken. Paying the mortgage. None of those things seemed right here, and yet, *something* was required. "Sam…if I was the dating ty—"

"If you tell me you're not interested in relationships again," she whispered, "I'm going to add another three bottles of Mountain Dew to this basket. And I'm not going to let you carry it to the check out for me."

A rumble left Duke's throat. *Ouch.* How did this girl know him so well after less than twenty-four hours? "That's not what I was going to say."

"Well, hurry up and state your purpose." She winced. "This basket is getting heavy."

"*Sam.*"

"Gotcha."

His heart ramped up speed. At this rate, he'd end up in the emergency room before he got his first bite of ribeye. Better get this horrible decision over with so he could begin to plan for the fallout. He couldn't see a way around going home and being preoccupied with her well-being all day, unless he did this. "Come to my place. I'm grilling."

Her serene expression remained in place. "Next time, I think I'll draw you in a straitjacket."

Fair enough. Might even be an accurate depiction by the

time she left Hook. "Speaking of straitjackets, my sisters are going to be there." He tried to be subtle about taking the junk food laden hand basket from her, but she blocked him. "You know you want to draw them," he gritted out.

Samantha waffled before his eyes. Adorably, of course. She couldn't help the pursing of her pink lips, the mixture of censure and excitement transforming her features, any more than *he* could help wanting to tangle their tongues together again. See how high she could climb this time before he came to his senses. Senses? Right. He'd waved good-bye to those when he'd asked her to his house. To eat his cooking, sit her sweet, spankable ass on his chairs, meet his friends and family. God, he must be out of his ever-loving mind.

"Why are you doing this?" Samantha asked, seriousness lacing her tone. "All we have to do is leave this store separately, go home, and…forget, right?"

A valid question. And one for which he couldn't provide an answer. There had been a few key moments in Duke's life—most of them overseas with the Army or during a particularly brutal machine repair—where he'd been required to trust his instincts. And his instincts were at full volume, warning him he'd regret leaving Samantha standing in that aisle with an armful of junk food. That he wouldn't *forget*. Maybe he just needed a little more time to accept his own reminder that a woman wasn't in the cards for him. She would come over, they would have a few laughs, agree to put the kiss from last night behind them….and part as friends.

Sure thing, asshole.

He forgot how to breathe as gravity tugged their gazes together, the connection snapping with energy he damned for being undeniable. "It's just a barbeque, Sam. It'll be fine."

A beat passed. Another one. "I'm being irresponsible with food because I just broke off my engagement. A few days ago."

Duke swore his insides turned to stone at her words. Cold, hard, ready to crumble stone.

"It's not what you think. He's been living out of the country for three years and…look, it's complicated. But I didn't feel a thing when I ended it. So I'm going through this one breakup ritual because I *should* have felt the slightest *something* when breaking a commitment. You know? Everyone should."

He watched as she pushed the fall of brown hair back over her shoulder, all of it happening at half speed. Breakup ritual? Did that account for their kiss last night? Had he been some kind of rebound make out session? Oh, fuck that. He really did not appreciate the possibility. *At all.* If he'd gone upstairs and made love to her, would she have been pining away over some other dude afterward?

Let's not get crazy. She would have been seeing stars when it was over.

That thought got everything moving in real time again, but he still wasn't appeased in the slightest. Not even when she tilted her head and smiled up at him.

"So…what should I bring to the barbeque?"

• • •

What on Earth was she doing back in this man's truck?

Answer: being a *moron*.

Samantha knew the score with Duke. He was playing the hero again, physically incapable of letting the poor damsel on aisle three go home without the proper nutrition. Oh no. Not with a mighty, penis-wielding warrior in the vicinity. She could have been anyone—*any* woman—and he'd have reacted the same. And that shouldn't cause a stab of sadness beneath her ribs. It definitely shouldn't.

Knowing Duke had a penchant for being a savior, she should have stuck to her guns and marched home, Cheetos in tow. Truthfully, though? When she'd unloaded on him about her broken engagement, it had felt so…nice. In three years, she could count on one hand the people to whom she'd imparted her impending marital status, and most of those times had been out of necessity. *I can't schedule the meeting for November…I'm getting…married?*

Yeah, the news always came out sounding like a question. Every time. At first, there had been something nice about knowing the future. Until that future had sped way too close to the present.

Duke hadn't spoken to her since she'd revealed her broken engagement, his jaw bunched so tight it would probably crack if she tapped it with her fingernail. She'd come along hoping to unburden herself further—and to catch a peek at these sisters—but a heart to heart didn't seem to be on Duke's agenda. Explaining cold feet to a man who would probably rather swallow bleach than walk down the aisle had made sense back at the supermarket, but perhaps she'd misjudged the situation.

"I really hate showing up without at least a six-pack—"

"Engagement," Duke growled. "Talk."

"O-kay." Samantha reached into the satchel on her lap, laying a hand on her sketchpad. "His name is Hudson—"

Snort.

"Really?" She waited for Duke to make a remark in English, but his eyes remained on the road. "All right, I'm going to start from the beginning, but I won't go into a ton of detail. Ready?"

Duke stayed silent. Shock of the century.

Samantha blew out a breath. "My brother—Renner…he kept me in the divorce. Between my mother and his father. He didn't just drop me, like he could have. And his support put me through college, and…it means a lot to me. I wouldn't have a career I love without him." She pushed her thumb into the spiral of her notebook, hard enough to distract her from the encroaching emotions. "I met one of Renner's investors, Hudson, my final year in college. We dated for two months, he asked me to marry him the night before he left for a three-year project in northern Yemen, and I said yes. I said...yes."

"Did you love him?"

She glanced over to double check Duke wasn't being strangled by his seatbelt, because that's how it sounded. "I don't remember," Samantha muttered. "I remember it made my brother happy. It meant strengthening their business partnership and bringing me into the enterprise. The united, married face of operations. Which is something Renner can't do effectively...at least not in the field of manufacturing."

One of the reasons she admired her brother so much was his refusal to hide his true self or make others comfortable for the sake of doing business. When their parents married, Renner—a teenager at the time—had already come out as gay. He lived according to his own rules, but those rules didn't always jive with the business arena he'd chosen. That's where Samantha and Hudson were going to come in. She consoled herself with the belief that she couldn't compromise her own happiness to make business run smoothly, but nothing helped. Not even anger at the unjust maneuvering of her life in the first place. By breaking off the engagement, she'd let Renner down, no matter how she looked at the situation.

"I knew having a bigger role in the company was part of the appeal for Hudson, and I thought, good. Fine. I'm being useful to Renner, who didn't give up on me when it counted. But, love?" She sighed. "I don't remember. I watched my mother marry and divorce twice. Renner's father...heck, I've lost count of which wife he's on. Isn't making someone happy, someone who's shown you kindness, a decent enough reason for saying yes to marriage? It's a better reason than most people could give."

Duke took a turn, bringing them down a narrow residential street. It was so lush with greenery Samantha sat forward in her seat, taken by surprise. Little kids played basketball at the far end, tossing the orange ball through a hoop on wheels. Girls sat huddled together on the sidewalk, Band-Aids on their knees, whispering. Probably about the boys. Neighbors stood in groups on the lawns, gesturing with great big sweeps of their hands, laughing loud enough that Samantha could hear it in the car. Were they even in Hook anymore?

She was reeled back to the conversation when Duke cleared his throat. "So why break the engagement? What changed?"

"He scheduled his flight home." She could see the email in her mind's eye. A forwarded itinerary from Virgin Airlines, with a winky face emoji as the entire accompanying message. Over the three-year separation, she'd spoken to Hudson once a week on Saturdays, and every so often, she let it go to voicemail. A fact that had forced a revelation. Speaking with her fiancé was a chore. She was marrying a virtual stranger. And *none* of it had to do with her own happiness.

Being engaged had been a convenience. In addition to strengthening the manufacturing business, it gave Samantha an excuse not to put herself out there. No dating meant no breaking up. No downward spiral, no dividing of possessions or friends. Through the engagement, she'd even fooled herself into believing she had a healthy attitude toward relationships. She'd said yes to marriage, after all. Maybe she'd gotten through a youth spent swapping households unscathed. Her own lies had been exposed when that email hit her inbox, though, and panic dropped like a heavy theater curtain.

"It wasn't pretend anymore, once he scheduled the flight. And I freaked." Samantha reached over and laid a hand on Duke's tense shoulder. "See? You had nothing to worry about this whole time. I'm just as big a commitment-phobe as you."

Of course, she'd never felt such an insane pull toward anyone—especially a man—in her life. Even now, she wished for darkness so she could edge closer, hoping he would wrap one of those beefy arms around her waist, haul her into his big, safe lap. God, he smelled good this morning. Less beer and sweat, more fabric softener and shaving foam. *Looked* good, too, for all the bluster in his dark expression. His light colored jeans were old and faded, too thin to keep the brawn of his thighs a mystery. Since he stared straight ahead, appearing deep in thought, Samantha let her gaze move inward, where his bulge rested on the seat. And yeah, okay, she hadn't imagined his…girth last night. Holy God.

You're a piece of work, Waverly. Judging the size of a man's genitals while discussing your broken engagement.

"See something you want to get a closer look at, sweetheart?" Heat rushing to the top of her head, Samantha's attention snapped up to find Duke watching her beneath hooded eyelids. "No? Then I suggest you get back on your side of the truck."

Uh…when had she slid closer? The leather seat was warm and smooth against her thighs as she retreated to the passenger side. It was then she realized the car no longer moved. "Are we here?"

"Yes, but we're not done talking."

"Really? Wow. Your vocal cords must be in shock."

Duke's mouth moved into a flat line. "This meeting on Monday with Bastion. What's it about?"

He'd been paying close attention, and that shouldn't have sprung a garden full of flowers to life in her stomach, but it did. She also wasn't ready to speak the reason for her meeting with Renner out loud. Not yet. Because while the broken engagement hadn't hurt? Breaking up with her dream business—one she'd been working to make a reality since discovering a passion for illustrating in college—would be like sawing off a limb.

"Why do you want to know all this?" she asked, curiosity a relentless tug at her consciousness. "It has nothing to do with you."

A hint of honest to goodness confusion crossed his face before he went back to being made of stone. Why was she asking such leading questions in the first place? Perhaps her motives weren't intentional, but they were there nonetheless. She didn't want to be the only one experiencing the tangible attraction between her and Duke. It was possible she wanted some sign she wasn't alone. A dangerous, pointless mission she wasn't in the right head space to be on.

Resolving to get through the barbeque and bounce, Samantha intentionally lost the staring contest with Duke, pushing open the passenger side door. And freezing. "Is that your *house*?"

"Yeah," Duke answered, rounding the truck's front bumper. "What about it?"

"It…" She pointed up at the tall, three story masterpiece atop a grassy hill. "It looks like a ship."

Without having eyes on Duke, she could still picture him tilting his head and squinting. "I don't see it."

"You don't—" Samantha dropped into a crouch, snagging the sketchpad from her satchel. Of course, it opened to the drawing she'd done last night of Duke, in a black mask, holding a sign that read KISS BANDIT. "Um…don't worry about that. Look here." Ignoring Duke's grumble, Samantha sketched the bare bones of Duke's house. Beside it, she formed the prow of a ship, pencil scraping and diving and cornering. "That grass knoll is like an ocean wave. And that balcony, it's the helm, where the captain stands. That's your bedroom, isn't it?"

He confirmed with a grunt. "I guess the chimney could be the crow's nest."

She raised her sketchpad in the air, like she'd just won

Olympic gold. "*Yes.*" Oh God, satisfaction swept Samantha down to her toes, the kind that only happened when someone confirmed she wasn't destined for the asylum. "Sea captain," she breathed with a nod, sliding the pad back into her bag. Feeling Duke watching her, she looked up from behind her fall of hair.

His eyes might as well have been shooting fire, that humungous chest shuddering up and down. "You make everything look different."

The sun suddenly shone brighter. "Thank you."

"I don't like changes."

"I have no plans to make any," Samantha returned, hating the way her wayward hope dimmed, when it shouldn't exist at all. Swallowing the thickness in her throat, she gripped the strap of her satchel and turned for the house. "I like my steak medium."

Chapter Five

Duke was in a *bad* place. Summer Saturday barbeques were usually his version of paradise. He stood at the grill with a cold beer, listened to sports radio, and once everyone passed on their order, they left him the hell alone. Well, not today. Today he'd brought along a woman who, until a few days ago, had been promised to another man—knowledge that basically made him want to rip up the backyard's brick patio with his bare hands—and how was he supposed to focus on cooking meat, when thoughts of Samantha in a wedding veil were flashing like mortar fire around his head?

I'm just as big a commitment-phobe as you. No, he'd wanted to shout at her. *No, you're perfect for someone.* Who wouldn't jam a ring down on the finger of such a beautiful, intelligent, funny-to-boot woman and say their vows at top speed, just in case she changed her mind? An idiot, that's who. An idiot like Duke.

So be it. He'd never claimed to have the answers to life. But his decision to remain a single man until death called his number didn't mean he could appreciate thoughts of

Samantha…married. Unreachable. Off the market. Sleeping with—

Oh no. *Not* going there. Not imagining her crawling into some strange bed, wearing garter belts and one of those silky deals, tan all over from her honeymoon. *Honeymoon?* Was he trying to kill himself? Knowing she dated someone for two months—*three years ago*—was like pouring acid into fresh wounds, then lighting them on fire. And if she hadn't broken off the engagement, Duke never would have met her at all. She would have been off in Manhattan, married to some guy who'd left her alone and unprotected for three years, Duke never being the wiser. Which would have been good, right?

Right…

Here was what he needed to focus on: the new proof of his theory's correctness, which Samantha's story had handily provided. No one in her life had stayed together, either. Unfortunately, the proof didn't make him feel validated. No, it was having the opposite effect. It made Duke want to prove the opposite of his theory. Because it was one thing for Duke to be a cynical bastard, and quite another for Samantha to believe happiness couldn't be achieved. He didn't want to live in a world where Samantha's betrayal was inevitable. Because if that were true, everything else was a fucking sham.

"How are you going to introduce me?" Samantha asked now, as they paused at his front door. "Do they hate Renner, too?"

Duke inserted his key in the lock, turning. "Never said I hated him."

"Your silence on the subject was deafening." He opened the door, indicating Samantha should precede him, which she then did. "I'd rather just be the girl you met at The Third Shift. It doesn't feel like a lie of omission, since they'll only know me for today."

Hell, she didn't have to sound so *breezy* about it. "Sure.

I won't mention it." Duke stood poised inside the entrance, watching Samantha float through his foyer, into the living room. After watching her conjure up alternate personalities for him and imagine his house as a ship, Duke wondered if she would see knickknacks or far more exciting objects with deeper meaning. What would she think of his Army Commendation Medal that one of his sisters had put in a glass case on the mantel?

Samantha ran her fingers over the display, turning a proud smile on him, and Duke just about lost the ability to breathe. He was way too damn curious about what she might say, so he shook himself and joined her in the room, watching as the hem of her dress trailed over his couch cushions. His johnson swelled. God, what would it be like? To have the freedom to lower Samantha to the couch, hold her knees wide open, and give her a hot, rowdy, afternoon fuck? He'd rip her right out of that little summer dress to get at those tits. Christ, if Duke gave in to the appetite she stirred in him, he probably wouldn't give a shit if the backyard was full of his sisters, either. His woman would get her satisfaction when, where, and how she needed it. Everyone else could deal.

His woman?

"You okay?" From her position at the window overlooking his backyard, Samantha was watching him over her shoulder. "Maybe you should put the steaks in the fridge?"

"Yeah." His voice sounded like a rust bucket. "The backyard is through the kitchen. Come on."

While following his directive, she shook her head. "Do you order all your guests around?" Duke frowned as he followed her into the kitchen. "Never mind. Just...try not to get used to it," he heard her say.

Duke wasn't given a chance to ask for clarification on that ominous comment—and whether she'd been talking to him or herself—because the Sister Apocalypse was upon them.

As soon as he and Samantha entered the backyard, they descended like vultures.

"Oh!" Luanne, the oldest, stood first, gin and tonic held aloft. "Who's this?"

"A girl? Is that a girl? Am I dead?" Lisa. The second youngest. "Did I die? Am I floating around in some alternate universe right now? Look at the dress, would you please? That is a fuckin' *dress*."

All four of them teetered across the patio, walking on tiptoe for no reason Duke could figure. "Luanne, Lorraine, Lisa, Lacey…this is Sam." He nudged her forward with his shoulder. "Go easy on her. She's from Manhattan."

"Wait wait wait wait whoa whoa whoa. Is this a date?" Lisa again. She spoke mostly in question format. "Do we have front row tickets to our big brother's *date*?" She popped a lit cigarette back into her mouth. "I'm a wreck. I'm dead."

Luanne jumped back in, ice cubes clinking together in her drink. "How much was that dress? Never mind. Don't tell me." She swatted a bug out of the air. "God. It's fuckin' *hot* out here."

Just when Duke was starting to become worried by Samantha's silence, she turned to him, beautiful face awash in awe and excitement. Her smiling lips were parted, fingers busy on the strap of her bag. That was all he got, though. A glimpse. Then his sisters were dragging her toward the patio, shoving her down into a deck chair.

"What do you drink?"

"Vodka? You probably drink vodka and diet something, you skinny bitch."

Samantha laughed as his name-calling sister hip-bumped her chair, softening the insult with a wink. "Anything. Yes. All of it." That earned her a cheer, making her smile grow even brighter. "You guys can try the dress on, if you want."

"Whoa. Time out." Duke cut a hand across his neck. "Two

things. One. This isn't a date. She was buying Mountain Dew and Cheetos at the market. And that's *all* she was buying." Gasps all around from his family, which was pretty goddamn gratifying. "Two. No one is taking any dresses off. Are we clear?"

"Big brother," Lacey, the youngest, sing-songed. "I don't think you get the point of dating."

"Not a date."

Duke smirked as they all got a big chuckle at his expense. Nothing he wasn't used to. The women went back to talking, which should have signaled Duke's usual escape to Grill Utopia, but his feet were stuck in place, watching his sisters buzz around a glowing, animated Samantha. Besides Bastion, did Samantha have any siblings? Why hadn't he thought to ask? She didn't seem accustomed to so many personalities being thrown at her at once, but damn it all if she wasn't taking everything in stride. Her responses were stilted and unsure at first, but in minutes, an outsider would swear she'd been there all along. Sitting on his patio.

He'd become so focused on cataloguing Samantha's mannerisms—her head ducking when she laughed, fingers sliding back and forth at her neckline while someone relayed a story—Duke didn't hear Vaughn approach until his ex-Army buddy and co-worker at the factory shoved him forward a step, having just left the guest house above his garage. "Are you sick or something, man? It's past noon and the grill isn't lit."

"Get a beer and shut up," Duke growled, slightly thrown off by how long he'd stood there, unaware of time passing.

Good humor still in place—it *always* was now that he'd married his high school sweetheart, River—Vaughn fished a Bud out of the ever-present cooler adjacent to Duke's grill. Even in a town he'd lived in since birth, there weren't many men Duke called "friend." No, *acquaintances* were more his speed. Knew everyone but kept to his own business. Vaughn refused to stay a mere acquaintance, however, and Duke suspected it went both ways, since he never went out after work with the other factory workers, either. Since returning to Hook and winning back River, Vaughn had secured a job as head of security at the factory. Not an easy feat, either, considering he'd gone through Renner Bastion to get there.

"Who's the girl, you big, dirty tomcat?" Vaughn asked.

"I'm going to poison your steak."

"Really? I thought brute force was more your thing." The other man took a pull from his bottle, condensation already making tracks down the brown glass. "Come on. River is on her way down. You know she'll get it out of you, sooner or later."

"Darn right I will," River murmured, coming up behind Duke and then laying a smacking kiss on his cheek. "So? Who is she?"

Duke turned a knob and watched the flames marry over the grill. "Met her at The Third Shift," he said, fighting the itch to catch Samantha's eye, make sure she was all right. "Look, it's just a barbeque. Don't make a big deal out of it."

River arched a blond eyebrow, staring off toward the gathering of women. "You met *her* at The Third Shift?"

"What's she in Hook for?" Vaughn's gaze was speculative. "She can't be visiting family. Unless—"

"Drop it." A beat passed. Followed by a low whistle from Vaughn and a drawn out *ohhhh* from River. "Great. That took all of thirty seconds," he said. "Yeah, all right. She's Bastion's stepsister. Act like you don't know."

"Why?" River asked.

"Because she knows we're not exactly planning on nominating Bastion for sainthood. She wants to be judged fairly."

Vaughn cocked a hip, holding the bottle of beer to his

mouth. "Is she anything like her brother?"

"Hell no, she isn't," Duke blustered. "She's sweet as all get out. You should see the way she gets in and out of my truck, it's—" He cut himself off when both friends gave another low whistle, this time simultaneous. "It's just a barbeque."

Both River and Vaughn's jaws were in the vicinity of their feet, but thankfully Duke didn't have to complete the interrogation, because a tiny blond blur came streaking down from the guest house, shouting his name. *"Duuuuuuke!"*

• • •

The world stopped revolving.

As Duke scooped up the blond child who careened at him full speed, tossing her up into the air, Samantha actually rose to her feet, the way one does at the end of a symphony with the intention of applauding. Around her, the conversation continued without a hitch, but she couldn't say the same for her pulse. It performed some offbeat version of Morse code, *bap bapbapbap bap bap*.

What danger was this?

Turn back, turn back.

But no. Samantha ran straight into the eye of the storm, watching the adorable blond kid wrap her paint-streaked arms around Duke's linebacker neck, cupping her hands around his ear, sharing a secret. Oh, and then he had to laugh, husky shoulders shaking, eyes crinkling at the corners.

Mayday. Mayday.

Someone—Lacey—tugged on her hand. "You all right, Sammy?"

"What? Yes." She reached for her drink where it sat in the chair's cup holder, coating her suddenly parched throat with refreshing flavors of vodka, soda, and lime. "Is that Marcy?"

Luanne sucked in a smiling breath. "She's here?" In

perfect tandem, all four sisters stood and jogged on tiptoes toward the barbeque, same as they'd done with her ten minutes earlier. "Marcy, come over here and meet your Uncle Duke's date."

"It's not a date," Samantha called—super lamely and high-pitched—trading an awkward wave with River and Vaughn. Then promptly draining her drink. Two sisters commandeered little Marcy, while the others rounded up the child's parents, guiding them to where Samantha stood on the patio. "They said it couldn't be done!" Luanne beamed at Samantha, jerking her forward by the elbow. "River, Vaughn, this is Samantha. We're going to lock her in the basement until Duke pulls his head out of his ass."

"I heard that," Duke groused, tossing steaks onto the grill, creating a loud sizzle and pop. "Watch your mouths in front of Marcy."

Luanne eye-rolled her brother while Samantha shook hands with the newcomers. "So nice to meet you. I'm…it's really not a—"

"Date," River supplied, smiling warmly in a way that put Samantha at ease right away. "They're going to call it whatever they feel like. Roasting the guest is kind of a Crawford family tradition."

"I'm picking up on that." Samantha laughed, receiving a firm shake from Vaughn, who appeared reluctant to remove his arm from around River's shoulders for even that brief second.

Samantha crouched down to get eye level with Marcy, holding out her hand. "How do you do?"

A blush moved up Marcy's neck, but she managed the shake. "Hi."

Samantha nodded at her colorful arms. "Are you a painter?"

"Yes."

"Her canvas is every surface in the guest house," Vaughn said, humor and pride blending in his tone. "Good thing Duke didn't ask for a security deposit."

"Especially since we'll be moving soon." River leaned into Vaughn. "We just had our offer accepted on a house."

"Get out of town!" Lorraine yelped, liquor sloshing over the rim of her drink.

"Oh, we'll still be in town," River murmured, smiling up at her husband. "Only five houses down, actually."

"I'm dead. I'm dead again. What is this? Today is my funeral, or what?" Lisa pressed two fingers to her temple, breathing as if she'd gone into labor. "We're going to need champagne. This is ridiculous."

Samantha found herself sharing a chair with Marcy a moment later as everyone else descended into a conversation about interest rates and inspections and who in town was looking to unload furniture. "What's that?" Marcy asked, pointing at Samantha's bag, where the corner of her sketchpad was visible.

"I was hoping you'd ask me that," Samantha said. "I have a really fun idea. Would you like to hear it?"

A vigorous nod. It never got old when kids reacted that way. No hesitation. Just yes to fun. Yes to the unknown. That leap without looking mentality had attracted Samantha to children's books and ultimately...her passion project. The project she'd been working since college to breathe life into.

Art on Wheels had started as an idea she'd voiced to Renner one afternoon over lunch in Manhattan. She loved illustrating, but she'd only landed on the interest by chance. So many kids who possessed a talent for art would never know it. So why not bring it to their attention? Perhaps hers was a fanciful business model—a fact she made no apologies for, because what was art if not occasional whimsy? Bringing a mobile art studio neighborhood to neighborhood, sending in artists to volunteer their time to children...it was her dream. Art on Wheels meant organizing special school events during which students would be free of assignments, allowed to express without constraint. Creating art. Maybe discovering a talent that had almost passed Samantha by.

Then she'd taken it a *giant* step further. Instead of simply sharing art locally, she'd thought, why not make it nationwide? So she'd started a network of artists online, through a self-designed website, all of whom were waiting to mobilize their own leg of Art on Wheels in seventeen different cities across the Unites States. Like most artists, however, everything hinged on funding. Crowd-sourcing had been an option, but she hadn't wanted to lose any control of the direction.

Upon approaching Renner, she'd expected him to shrug the project off as non-feasible or some other buzzkill business term. But he hadn't. To her astonishment, Renner had agreed to co-sign on Samantha's bank loan, get it off the ground. He'd believed in it, as he'd believed in *her,* when no one else did. Unfortunately, as with anything Renner-related, there were conditions. And as Samantha didn't meet those conditions anymore, she knew the funding would no longer be happening. A fact she would confirm on Monday.

Samantha shook herself when she realized Marcy was watching her expectantly. "Um, okay. Here's the idea. You tell me a story. *Any* story in your head, and I'll draw it..." She slipped out her sketchbook, flipping open to a blank page. "Right here. When we're done, it'll be like we wrote a short book together. Okay?"

Marcy nodded, propping her chin on a fist. "Uhhh..."

"What about your new house? Tell me what your room will look like."

The little girl's eyes widened to the size of silver dollars. "There's gonna be a pool..."

After Marcy's trust had been earned, it was smooth

sailing. As usual, when she had a pencil in hand, Samantha faded out, along with her surroundings. The conversation taking place quieted to a hum, overridden by the comforting *scratch scratch scratch*. Marcy's shy voice was a welcome addition as they worked together to create the ultimate fairytale bedroom. Monkeys hung down from the ceiling, princesses had their own special door, the bed transformed into the pool with a wave of a magic wand. Butterflies were everywhere. And since they were having such a good time, Samantha started on the backyard and a roof garden chock full of fairies and kitty cats.

"Someday, I hope I can go into schools and draw stories for lots of kids," Samantha said. "Do you think they would like that?"

"Yes," Marcy breathed, propping her chin on her crossed forearms.

"It would be a whole day, just for making *stuff*..."

Samantha lost track of time passing as she talked to Marcy. She finished and held the drawings out to the little girl. It took a moment to regain her equilibrium, but when finally she did, they'd been cast in a massive shadow. Samantha tipped her head back, expecting to find storm clouds, but instead found Duke watching from behind the chair, arms criss-crossing his chest. Marcy leaped off Samantha's lap, drawings clutched in her fists, off to show them to her parents, but Duke didn't seem inclined to stop staring any time soon. So Samantha stared right back, even though it pained her neck.

"See something you want to get a closer look at, sweetheart?" Samantha asked, her voice dropped down into a Duke-style grumble.

His growl was for her ears alone, communicating his displeasure over having his earlier question repeated back. "Everyone's done eating and you haven't even started yet." He tilted his head toward the house. "Have yours warming in the oven. Come on."

With his sisters still holding an in-depth discussion with River and Vaughn, the latter of whom now held Marcy propped on his hip, Samantha followed Duke to the kitchen. Entering the quiet, empty room resulted in a blast of intimacy. Since Duke had his back turned, removing her plate from the oven, she couldn't tell if he felt it, too. Neither could she get a read on him when he turned and dropped her plate on the counter with a clatter. And then…

…Duke crooked his finger at her. And hell seemed to break loose between them, filling the air with blazing energy.

"Sorry, what's that?"

"That's the international signal for get over here," he rasped.

Samantha wasn't given to crashing waves of arousal. No, her libido could more accurately be described as a tide pool, at least *before* she'd met a certain machinery mechanic. But something about that finger, the absolute gall, the male *ego* behind it, tossed her around like a pissed off ocean. Duke was turned on. The testosterone was a veritable force field around him, and Samantha wanted in. Hadn't it been inevitable when they'd met again this morning, so soon after last night? And was she making excuses, telling herself that giving over her body was safe? This was physical, right here. They could touch each other in his kitchen and she'd still be going home when the waves stopped pounding. No other option. Especially leaving without another sample of what had made her feel so…*alive*. "If I come to you, what are you going to do when I get there?"

"I'll tell you one thing…" If possible, Duke's size seemed to double, his muscles shifting beneath his T-shirt. "It's going to involve your mouth."

Chapter Six

It's going to involve your mouth.

Now *that's* what Duke called hedging his bets. Because by bringing Samantha into the kitchen, he'd aimed to feed her. Right. He'd seen through his own excuse the moment they stepped foot through the door and canceled out the background noise, leaving nothing but the sound of that sexy dress swishing, Duke's own jeans rubbing together between his thighs. *Goddamn.* Her tits were rosy from the sunshine, telling him they'd be warm against his palms. Due to his size, a large kitchen had been a necessity when house shopping all those years ago, but it closed in now, dwindling the six feet of distance between them to nothing.

Out in the backyard, Samantha had been nothing short of…spellbinding. And hell, he'd never said that word out loud *in his life*. No other description seemed to do her justice, though. Ankles crossed, mouth smiling, head nodding, hair sticking to her neck as she spoke so dreamily about her dream of bringing art to children. How he'd kind of wanted to pick up the world and demand it give Samantha what she wanted.

To stop making her sound sad about *any* damn thing.

And God…that body, *always* that body, posed in such a way that sex infiltrated his brain like a fucking SWAT team, fanning out and pointing flashlights at impulses he'd kept in check for so long. Impulses that had *never* been this strong. Not for anyone. *Jesus Christ,* he was so hard, his teeth gritted of their own accord to battle the ache.

His cock, wedged up behind his belt, was crying out for the pink flesh Samantha was hiding under her dress, his hips thrusting back and forth—just an inch—in mid air. Somehow between last night and this afternoon, he'd turned into a hungering animal, and there didn't seem a way to quit that behavior.

Not without appeasing it, at least. Just the suggestion set his swollen flesh pulsing. Which was dangerous as hell, because Duke didn't think with his dick. Ever. And if his brain held the required amount of blood for rational thought, he would remind himself that Samantha deserved better than a hookup with a fellow commitment-phobe, as she'd termed their condition, and to walk away with a memory.

A really hot, satisfying memory.

No, she deserved to be cured and think positively about relationships. He was an old dog who couldn't learn new tricks. But not Samantha. Not this bright, beautiful sweetheart walking toward him, expectation in her big doe eyes.

Maybe Duke was only delaying the inevitable, but when Samantha glided close enough, he swung her up onto the counter instead of into his arms. Where was the relief that usually followed averted disaster? *Move your ass, relief.*

"Oh," Samantha whispered when Duke forked a piece of steak, holding it to her mouth. "I guess chewing involves my mouth, doesn't it? Womp womp."

"Eat."

"Presumtu—" He cut her off by placing the bite in her

moving mouth, earning a glare from Samantha. "I can feed myself," she said, after swallowing.

"That's debatable."

Her shoulders bunched, eyes firing, and she moved closer, ready to deliver an insult, Duke guessed. And *hoped*. Maybe if they fought, it would distract him from tits he could only describe as playful, within reaching distance of his hands. "I like your family and friends," Samantha grated instead.

Duke leaned down to get in her face, dropping the fork as he went. "Oh yeah? They like you, too."

"I'm having a *lovely* time."

"Good," he growled. "You're so fucking beautiful under the sunshine I can't stop looking at you."

"Well…" She speared him in the chest with a finger. "I can't stop looking at you and your big ox shoulders, either." Her breath escaped in a rush. "This was a terrible idea. I'm going to make like a banana and leave."

God save me, she's adorable. Did she always mix up her puns when she was nervous? Somehow they'd moved closer, their lips brushing as Duke spoke. "I'll call you a cab."

"Good."

"Fine."

Everything that *needed* to happen was all spelled out, but when Samantha actually made a move to climb off the counter, Duke's body decided on a different course of action—and his body was adamant. He threw her over his shoulder like a caveman before her feet could touch the ground and then stormed toward the front hallway that led to his bedroom. Couldn't be anything wrong with this. They were two adults who didn't want anything serious from one another, acting on urges. Urges that weren't going to subside no matter how much logic he attempted to drown them in.

Samantha had other ideas.

"Put me down."

"Soon as we get to where we're going."

"*Ohhh?* Where's that?"

She was speaking through gritted teeth, which probably should have been a warning. As soon as he took another step, he felt Samantha's hand slip into the back of his jeans, wrangling a fist full of underwear...and then the little hellcat—had he actually referred to her as sweet?—gave him an honest-to-God wedgie.

"*Christ,*" Duke spat, removing her from his shoulder. She landed on her feet, a satisfied glint in her eye. "Did you just—"

"Yup."

More turned on by her juvenile strategy than was rational, Duke backed Samantha up against the hallway wall, a boulder of need shifting in his belly when she sucked in a breath, held it, those doe eyes wide enough to swim in. *That's right, sweetheart. You don't know what's coming.* "I can't see a way around fucking you, Sam. Giving it to you until you're a whimpering little mess."

Pink swarmed her cheek like bees. "You should quit your job and write poetry full time."

He smiled, but the ticking in his jaw made it feel unnatural. "If you didn't like the way I speak, your nipples wouldn't be poking me in the stomach right now."

"Maybe I'm cold," she breathed.

Duke stepped closer, flattening Samantha against the wall, leaning down to talk at her temple. "Maybe you're the hottest thing I've ever seen." He dropped an arm, sliding it beneath her ass and boosting her up. The tight proximity of their bodies caused the upper half of her dress to slide down, revealing two perfect mounds topped with raspberry-colored peaks. Duke's cock jerked with a surge of lust, fighting the fly of his jeans to gain freedom. There was something...corrupt about having an angry girl topless in his hallway while a party was in full swing outside. A girl whose eyes continued to spit fire at him, even though her inner thighs rubbed restlessly against his hips. "When men think of putting their mouths on a woman's tits, they don't picture themselves sucking gently. Or blowing on them." He rubbed the seam of his lips across one delicious looking tip. "Not me, anyway. Not since I've seen this pair you're walking around with."

"What do you want to do?" she asked, voice unsteady.

The nervous quality of her tone shouldn't have made his need more insistent, but lord, it did. Pretty thing, half naked in his dark hallway. *All for him.* "I want to show you how dirty they make me feel. I want to risk you being offended by the permission I'm going to take with them."

Their harsh inhales and exhales were the only sound alive in the hallway. That, and the quiet, rasping journey of Samantha's thighs up and down his hips. Duke waited a beat, hoping like hell she didn't ask to be put down. His cock was nothing short of engorged, damping his fly with every flicker of Samantha's eyelids, every tremble of her lips. Every ounce of Duke's focus went into reading her natural signals, so he almost missed the subtle nod she gave.

His mouth fell to her right nipple like a starving man finally given the go ahead to devour a sugar-topped pie. She strained under his rough suck, back arching, moan catching in her throat. *She's amazing.* The taste of her, the way she seemed to burst under the pleasure—pleasure *he* provided—was fucking incredible. And she struggled against it, against him. Pushing him away with her hands, holding him in place with her thighs. The mixed signals bashed at his control like a battering ram, heightening everything. The voices in the distance, her earlier irritation.

Duke released her accosted nipple with a loud pop, then—sending her a look of pure debauchery—he licked at it. Once, twice, before reaching up and slapping the slight weight of her breast, hard enough to make it shake, hard enough to earn him a feminine gasp. "Are you going to let me get away with that?" Duke rasped, lashing at her with his tongue, the flesh below his waist growing so thick he had to widen his stance to accommodate it. "You going to let me punish you for flirting with those men in the supermarket?"

Until the words left Duke's mouth, he didn't realize there'd been a hammering at the back of his skull since spotting her in the aisle that morning, surrounded by other men. Other cocks. And now that he acknowledged the possessive streak she'd awakened, he couldn't suppress it, couldn't stop it from curling around his neck like a boa constrictor and pulling taut. Samantha wasn't turned off by it, either. No, she threw her head back, tilting her body to display her tits fully, her body beginning a mind-fucking undulation against him. "I-I…" She caged a scream when Duke ground against her middle, jiggling those tits enough to triple the throbbing in his dick. "I wasn't—"

"You were. You don't even have to open your mouth, sweetheart." He grazed her left nipple with his bared teeth. "Soon as you put on this sexy-girl dress and make eye contact with a man, they think you're flirting. They get amped up, the way I'm amped up to fuck you into a stupor right now. And that makes me want to break their goddamn faces."

Rationality had taken a vacation. Didn't matter that minutes ago he'd said he would call her a cab. Honesty was at the helm now, steering his ship into dangerous waters, but there was nothing he could do to stop it. He was ashamed to admit there was even a fair amount of resentment toward Samantha for rousing these instincts. How dare she bonk her head off the bar and draw him like a gladiator and ruin everything. His solitude, his routine, his sanity. *Everything.*

Duke palmed Samantha's left breast, molding it roughly. They hit one another with blistering eye contact just before he lifted his hand and slapped her peaked nipple.

Samantha's palm cracked against his cheek, leaving

a stinging sensation in its wake. The retaliation he'd been hoping for in secret, because it would finally break this spell she'd cast over him. Right?

Wrong. If anything, now that she'd chastised him, too, he wanted—*needed*—to win her back. Apologize for being a jealous tool by orgasming her mind-blowing body until the sun rose tomorrow morning. "Goddammit, Sam," Duke groaned against soft, gasping lips. "You're doing a number on me."

"Same goes."

They went for one another's mouths at the same time, and Duke's lungs were instantly imbued with oxygen. His head cleared of confusion, because their tongues rubbing together and bodies pumping in unison left no room for questions. They were man and woman and lust, tangled together, slamming up against the wall, moaning and grunting, straining to get closer, hands grappling with clothes and zippers. Reason having hit the road ages ago, Duke actually pulled Samantha off the wall, turned, and rammed her up against the opposite hallway wall, simply to shock a gasp from her lips. Because he wanted to swallow it. Savor it. So he reared them back and did it again, grinding their lower bodies into the solid surface, until her legs began to quake around his hips.

"Duke." Her voice bounced along with her tits. *"Duke. Take me somewhere."*

"Has to be here," he growled into the crook of her neck. "I can't take my cock off you. Can't stop jacking myself on this hot pussy."

As if his body needed to prove the truth of his words, he thrust into her juncture hard enough to shake the wall, two side-by-side picture frames falling off their nails and tumbling to the floor.

"Oh my God." He felt Samantha's toes hook into his belt loops, the way they'd done last night, as she thrashed her head on the wall. "You're so hot. I can't believe how you kiss and this body, your body, it's so huge and hard and take me somewhere…am I saying all of this out loud. Who cares?"

Duke's heart tugged with such uncommon force, he collapsed onto Samantha, breathing in her scent to find balance, but only being knocked off farther. "You think I'm hot, huh?" Was that his voice? It sounded…unfamiliar. Distorted. "Hotter than those fuckers in the market?"

"What fuckers? What market?" Her head fell to one side, creating enough space to drag his open lips back and forth over her raging pulse. "Where am I?"

Incredible. His cock felt forged in steel and he still experienced the urge to laugh, to gather her close, feel the vibration of *her* laugh. And that impulse terrified him more than anything. It meant this connection with Samantha was more than sex. So why wasn't the sky falling yet?

"What do I do with you, sweetheart?"

Three heavy breaths. "What do we do with each other?" she whispered back.

"*Duke?*"

He and Samantha both stiffened at the sound of River's voice progressing closer through the kitchen. "Um. I've been elected to come in and tell you everyone is looking for seconds. Don't shoot the messenger."

When Samantha's legs unhooked from around his waist, Duke pinned her back against the wall with a snarl. *My woman is leaving me. She hasn't been tended to. I haven't done my job.* He only calmed when Samantha's smooth hands trailed up his chest, settling around his neck, massaging the tense muscles there. "Shhh."

Duke nodded reluctantly, although it was beyond him what it meant. That they would pick up where they'd left off later? Nothing had been resolved or decided, least of all where they stood. And that uncertainty was a bleeding stab wound in his jugular.

Finished fixing her clothes, Samantha turned to face River, just as the other woman appeared at the hallway's end, but Duke was forced to turn away, being that his dick was the size of an eggplant and all.

"I'm…" River paused, probably noticing the fallen pictures. "I'm sorry to interrupt, but Vaughn and I are leaving for Atlantic City in a couple hours. My brother's band has a show tonight and the sisters are babysitting Marcy." She cleared her throat, amusement and discomfort obvious in her voice. "We have an extra ticket, Samantha. I thought, since you were in town for the weekend, you might want to take it."

"Oh." Duke glanced over his shoulder to find Samantha flushed with pleasure. Not the kind he'd delivered but excitement over being included. His gut turned over in response, even as protests sprang to his lips. She continued before he could voice them, however. "That's…it's amazing of you to ask me. What's the band?"

Pride was evident in River's answer. "Old News."

"*Old News?*" Samantha's high-pitched squeal sent Duke into a mental eye roll. When living in Hook, hometown of the world famous band — and its lead singer Sarge Purcell — getting away from constant mentions of the band and the apparently good-looking front man continued to prove impossible. "I love them. Oh my God. Yes. Yes, I want to come. Thank you, River. I'll just have to run back to the apartment—"

"Hold up." Samantha's eagerness to leave Hook—and him—having put the kibosh on his erection, Duke finally turned to join the conversation. "You're not taking her to some loud, trashy casino and leaving her alone, while you and Vaughn drown yourselves in each other's eyes. Not happening." Duke's head dropped forward with a gale-force sigh, Bon Jovi's "Blaze of Glory" blaring in his head, because yeah, it appeared that's how he was going down. "You're not taking her, unless there's a fourth ticket for me."

Chapter Seven

Samantha's smooching high took a downward spiral when she saw the missed calls on her phone. She'd left it charging on her bedside table in the guest room of Renner's apartment all morning. All nine missed calls were from Renner, but he'd left not a single message, a strategy very like her brother. Just like his text message she'd received on the way into town, he clearly didn't want to tip her off to his mood or what methods he might employ to change her mind about the broken engagement. No, that would give her time to prepare, and he couldn't allow that. Seriously. She loved the man like they were real flesh and blood siblings, but he could be a jerk when he set his mind to it.

She fell back across the bed, cradling both cheeks in her hands. They were still on fire from the kiss with Duke. Would they ever go back to their normal temperature? God. *God.* An hour later, her jaw continued to unhinge every time she thought of his bruising treatment. The beastly drives of his hips, the growling, the slapping of her breasts, his coarse skin, the language he'd used. By the time Samantha finished making a mental tally of all the never-before-experienced moves, touches, and sounds, her thighs were clenched tight enough to meld together.

River was downstairs, waiting in the car for Samantha to pack an overnight bag, as they would be drinking tonight and didn't want to drive back to Hook. For the first time, she would be staying in a casino. Heck, it would be her first time in a casino at all. So…she *should* be throwing clothes into a bag, thrilled to not only see one of her favorite bands in a matter of hours, but also excited to *live*. Live outside her world of office walls and pencils and sketchpads.

Not that she was going to leave the sketchpad behind. Oh hell no.

Another thing she needed to pack? Her inhibitions. Investigating the attraction between her and Duke was one thing, but looking up into his deep, hooded eyes and asking *what are we going to do about each other?*

That was a horse of a different color. Like, puce. Or black, maybe. Because there was no doing *anything*. It was unrealistic to expect they could go an entire overnight trip without getting physical, but that's where their relationship would start and stop. Not only because genuinely liking him signaled potential disaster—*normal* people couldn't stick out relationships, let alone fully pledged commitment-phobes—but furthermore, Duke worked for Renner. Her perfectionist brother would be about as thrilled to find her dating an employee as he'd be to find his factory producing sex toys.

As in, he'd hit the roof.

She was only in Hook long enough to meet with Renner and apologize for breaking her commitment face-to-face instead of going through a lawyer. Because she knew too well what *that* felt like. Then she would ask him to reconsider co-signing the loan for Art on Wheels, even though she'd fallen short of his expectations.

It was a long shot. But one way or the other, she couldn't let her dream slip away so easily. Not when there were other artists nationwide, counting on her initiative. Not to mention the children that would benefit.

With one final dreading glance at her phone, Samantha unhooked the device from the charger and stowed it in her purse. It took less than five minutes to pack all the essentials—she hoped—for an overnight stay in Atlantic City. On her way out the door, Samantha stopped, though. When she'd left Manhattan, she'd been in dire need of doing laundry, so the emergency underwear she'd packed was…not her usual plain-colored bikini panties. They were bright neon pink and decorated with sparkles. She'd bought them as a pick-me-up one day when she'd felt particularly boring and sensible, modeling them once in her bathroom mirror, scoffing, taking them off…and wearing them only on the direst of laundry days.

Before Samantha could talk herself out of it, she snatched the panties up from the inner zipper pocket of her suitcase and shoved them into her overnight bag, then marched down the stairs a moment later to meet River.

The blond woman smiled, putting the car into reverse. "Got everything?"

"Yes," Samantha answered, trying to sound breezy, like a person who'd packed basic white underwear. "So, um…do you guys road trip to Atlantic City often?"

"Not at all." River sighed dreamily. "We've both been working nonstop, getting money together for the house. This is kind of a celebration trip."

"That's so nice," Samantha said, wedging the bag between her knees. "Are you sure I'm not intruding? I—"

"Oh no. No." River waved off her concern. "Actually, we're wondering if you're some sort of miracle worker, getting Duke to come along. He's going to miss SportsCenter tonight and everything."

Samantha's pulse kicked on with the force of a lawnmower, just hearing his name. *Hands. Big, abrasive hands.* "SportsCenter. Is that how he usually spends Saturday night?"

"No. It's how he spends *every* night. Well. When his sisters don't need something fixed. Or he's not cooking for them, or dealing with the fallout of an ill-advised phone call with an ex-husband of theirs." A beat passed. "Or he's not being called in on a late night repair at the factory. Or I'm not asking him to watch Marcy while I run to the store." River frowned. "Huh. Maybe he never actually gets to watch SportsCenter. Poor man."

"Yeah." Duke probably didn't even want to go to Atlantic City. Just like last night and this morning, he couldn't help piling obligations on his shoulders, whether he truly wanted them or not. Guilt was not something Samantha wanted to feel right now, but it remained at home in her gut, making her wonder if the trip was a mistake.

Wait a minute. Samantha straightened in her seat. She hadn't asked Duke to come along. He'd *demanded* the fourth concert ticket. Not to mention, he very likely would have found a way to keep her in Hook if that ticket hadn't been forthcoming. She wasn't allowed to have a good time if he wasn't there to grumble at her?

Presumptuous.

No more guilt. With a broken engagement and nine missed calls from Renner, she was feeling guilty enough already. Unfortunately, when River pulled up in front of Duke's house and tooted the horn, signaling the men to get ready with their luggage, the guilt roared back in full force. Duke stood on the front porch as they approached, speaking to his sisters in a concerned tone.

"All the numbers you might need are on the refrigerator,

okay? Pizza, emergencies, me." He ruffled his younger sister's hair. "Don't all run your hair dryers at the same time or the electricity will cut off. Since none of you will go in the basement to flip the breaker switch, that would be a problem, right? So, *coordinate*. For the love of God, coordinate your hair drying schedule. Just for one night."

"He's so worried about his baby sisters." Luanne reached up and gently slapped his cheek a few times. "Honey, I survived five years of marriage to an Italian man. I can survive anything."

He picked up a battered leather bag that made Samantha yearn to sketch him as a World War I soldier. Going off to the airbase, leaving his loved ones behind. Lord, by the time she finally decided on an alternate identity for Duke, she'd have ten pads full of him.

"Samantha, you take care of this guy, huh?" Lorraine patted him on the stomach. "Don't let him skip a meal, he turns into a bear."

An image of Duke's face on a bear's body sent a giggle sailing past her lips. "He becomes un*bear*able, you mean?" Silence. *Don't try again. Don't—* "Maybe he goes into Kodiak arrest?"

"I like her."

"Bring her back to us, big brother, or else."

With that, the sisters plucked a smiling Marcy out from between a hug sandwich made by her parents, then closed themselves in the house. *Click.* Their departure should have signaled Samantha to head for the car, but Duke's attention kept her pinned until she started to fidget.

"You know...you don't have to go," Samantha stage-whispered. "I don't need someone to keep an eye on me."

"Maybe I like the band."

"Name one song."

He threw the leather bag over his shoulder and cocked

TESSA BAILEY 79

a hip, in the sexiest, most masculine stance Samantha could have ever dreamed up. "You caught me. I'd rather listen to the Stones or Seger. All I know is I overhead Luanne calling Old News's songs 'panty droppers' in one of the most traumatic moments of my life." He sauntered forward, boots thudding on the porch. "So I'm coming, sweetheart. Because your panties aren't dropping unless I make them."

. . .

Thank Christ Atlantic City was only an hour drive from Hook, because Duke's leg was killing him from being cramped up in the back seat of River's red Pontiac. He wished that was the only member of his body giving him a problem, but it wasn't. In fact, somewhere around mile two, Duke had accepted that his cock would remain hard for all of time. Living with a full house, he'd learned to rub one out quickly in the shower before work most days, but that ritual no longer cut the mustard. Not with Samantha "I can't keep my legs still" Waverly sitting beside him in such close quarters.

At one point during the drive, she'd leaned down to retrieve the sketch pad from her overnight bag, giving him a view clear down the front of her dress. Which had been bad, for sure, but not the worst part. She'd removed the pad, placing it in her lap, without realizing a pink pair of fairy floss underwear were snagged in the metal spiral. Duke had lifted them with one finger, laughing when she turned beet red and shoved them back into hiding.

Laughter had been his only option, really, because otherwise he would have broken down in tears. Even Vaughn smirking at him in the rearview hadn't been able to coax enough anger to eclipse the arousal. The constant, brutal need he experienced around Samantha. The mere desire to find a bed and grind her body down into the mattress with his own?

Yeah, that wasn't where it ended, either. He wanted to watch her shower, see how she soaped her body. Wanted to listen to her talk—granted, while naked. And more than anything, Duke wanted to get right in Samantha's face and ask for the weight of her problems.

He *liked* to solve problems for those in his life, but this urgency prodding his throat—where Samantha was concerned—was new as hell. Fixing was something he'd always done. Because if he didn't repair the problem, no one would. Someone could get hurt or the problem could worsen. Fixing was his role and he took on issues the way a fisherman hauls the day's catch into a boat. With well-practiced movements and bleary-eyed registering of the outcome. A vast difference from the way a fire lit in his belly every time Samantha's forehead wrinkled in thought, every time he considered her being out of reach if her worries came to fruition.

Whatever those worries were.

Now, as Duke stood at the hotel check-in with Vaughn, he watched Samantha smile at something River said and brush that thick, gorgeous hair out of her face. When she'd left his house to pick up her things earlier, Duke had decided a solo sit-down-and-think was in order, so he'd doled out second helpings of barbeque'd meat to his sisters and closed himself in the master bedroom.

Twenty minutes of ruminating had produced a few conclusions. One, he didn't give a flying fuck if she was related to his boss. Perhaps he'd seen the drawbacks at first, but they'd been buried under a load of possessiveness that didn't appear ready to lighten any time soon. Two, he didn't have enough information when it came to the Monday meeting between Samantha and Renner. Which wasn't working for him. Three, if he didn't get inside her soon, his cock would jump ship, detach from his body, and make for greener pastures.

"Yo, Duke." Vaughn gave him an elbow in the ribs. "One

room or two?"

Reluctantly, he tore his eyes off Samantha. "What's that now?"

"You and Samantha. Same room, or—"

"Same room."

Vaughn appeared to be battling a smile at his expense. "Does she know that?"

Duke could already hear Samantha's gasp, followed by her husky delivery of *presumptuous*. Fuck, he'd love to hold the back of her head in one hand, his cock in the other, and hear that single word pass her lips just before his flesh dipped inside. See the accusation in her eyes as he pushed deep.

"Duke, you're creeping me out over here." Vaughn lowered his voice, probably so the hotel clerk couldn't hear their conversation. "Maybe you should get adjoining rooms or something. You don't want her thinking…you know…"

"What?"

His friend sighed, drumming a fist on the counter. "That it's a sure thing."

"No, I don't want her thinking that," Duke admitted with a frown. "Although, you're one to talk. Pretty sure you showed back up in Hook and pissed a circle around River. You sure as hell would have booked a single room."

Vaughn sent his wife a look so full of unabashed wonder, Duke had to glance away. "You're right about that." His finger prodded Duke in the chest. "But Riv and I had a history. So. Do as I say, not as I do."

"You weren't this wise when we were stationed together. It's annoying." A grumble shifted in Duke's throat. "Fine. Adjoining rooms." Once the clerk received the go ahead from Vaughn and the man's fingers started flying over the keyboard, Duke got another stern look from his friend. "Jesus. What now?"

"Hey, I'm just the well-meaning pal. And as such, I feel

duty-bound to point out…man, she's Bastion's sister." Vaughn hedged a little, clearly uncomfortable with the conversation but determined to press on. "Rich girl shows up looking for something new. Finds him. Then leaves guy to deal with the fallout while she skates off back to Manhattan. You've seen this movie. You know how it ends."

"With my job in jeopardy," Duke said with a grimace, leaning on the counter to ease pressure in his bad leg. "Crossed my mind and went out the other side. You've met her. She's nothing like that."

"That's my impression, too," Vaughn jumped in quickly. "But sometimes even the rich girl doesn't get a choice. So…" He cut the air with a hand, signaling an end to the talk. "Wits about you, that's all I'm saying."

Duke looked back at Samantha over his shoulder, heat sliding into its new favorite place—his groin—when she stared back at him, too. "Point taken," he said to Vaughn before turning back to hand the clerk his credit card.

Ten minutes later, they were upstairs in their rooms, Duke and Samantha two floors above River and Vaughn. Since Duke had no intention of dressing up for a concert, he'd thrown down his bag and set to pacing, hoping to alleviate the stiffness from his leg. Two hours remained before they'd planned to meet up with River and Vaughn. Duke had a damn good idea what his friends were getting up to about now, which accounted for the other reason he paced. Samantha was on the other side of a thin door, doing God knew what. Her hair or something, most likely. Women were always doing their hair and it never looked any different when they were finished.

What would happen if he knocked on the adjoining door? She would open it. And then what? He'd invite her in for tea?

Yeah, that sounded *just* like him.

Ah, Christ. He'd landed in the wooing phase by accident, hadn't he? Were men just built to act out of character to attract women, before they revealed their asshole nature beneath? Probably. His sisters and his mother had been duped and they were the smartest people he knew.

No different. You're no different.

Good thing Duke had his eyes open and could resist the urge to woo.

Right. He willed the door to just kind of...*tick*...open.

This could turn into a stalemate. Which wouldn't be happening if his "friend" Vaughn hadn't gotten into his head, forcing him to consider if Samantha's description of him— *presumptuous*—actually fit.

Duke dropped onto the bed with a curse, gaze locked on the door, like a bull waiting for a red flag to wave. This was why he stayed away from women, even so-called casual flings. Nothing was easy. Someone always walked away disappointed, wanting more, or all-out confused.

Confused was what Duke found himself half an hour later when a gentle knock sounded, coming from Samantha's room. "Duke?"

He was on his feet before realizing it. "What's wrong, sweetheart?"

A pause. "Why does something have to be wrong?"

"Something usually is."

Light shifted underneath the door. "Well." Suddenly, Samantha sounded pleased with herself and damn if that didn't baffle him further. He didn't have time to consider too closely, however, because she opened the door, sweeping to the side like a fancy maître-d, gesturing for him to enter. "Right this way, please."

"This feels like a trap."

Her nose screwed up, shoulders squaring as she opened her

mouth to reprimand him, no doubt…but then he heard it. The unmistakable—almost ethereal—sounds of SportsCenter. Holding his breath, Duke pressed a finger to Samantha's parted lips, bypassing her into the room. Highlights ran on the television like shiny offerings from heaven. *It's been so long.* Not only had she tuned to ESPN, but also the room was rearranged, the cushy armchair situated to face the television. But even convenient seating wasn't the icing on his highlight reel cake. Oh no. She'd ordered him a six-pack—either from room service or Valhalla—but whoever had brought the beer had delivered it in an ice bucket, leaving it beside the armchair.

"You did this for me?" God, he sounded like a chick. *Felt* like one, too, because…she'd turned the tables on him. She'd wooed before he could woo. *Stop saying "woo," jackass.* "Why?"

He turned to find Samantha hovering near the door, looking so nervous she reminded him of an electric toy store crystal ball, complete with neon energy crackling out from all sides. "Yeah, well. I, you know." She rested a hand on the door handle, but it dropped when Duke shook his head, starting toward her slowly. "River said you never get to watch it and that just seems unfair. Because you take care of everyone, even if—over the last twenty-four hours—I've been frequently annoyed by that quality. I'm annoyed right now, actually, because it's all I'm going to think about during the concert. Duke would rather be watching SportsCenter." He'd gotten within five feet of Samantha now, and she'd plastered herself up against the door. "So, like, go watch, right? What are you waiting—"

His mouth cut her off. The way she melted—like butter in a microwave—between his body and the door was fucking incredible, especially when he remembered she'd called him hot earlier. Him. *Hot.* Must have meant it, too, because when he pulled back her eyes were closed, head lolled back, arms slack at her sides. *Damn.* "Thank you, Sam."

"You're welcome," she whispered.

Duke stooped down to press his mouth beneath her chin. "We're going to fuck tonight. Your bed. Mine. On the floor. In the shower. Against the window. All. Goddamn. Night. You're going to know me from every angle when the sun comes up over New Jersey tomorrow." He took her knees, dragging that tight body up between himself and the door. "This might be the nicest thing someone's done for me. But frankly, sweetheart? When compared to you, SportsCenter can go fuck itself."

Overcome by hunger, Duke peeled Samantha off the door, making it to the bed in three long strides. She bounced once when Duke set her down, reminding him to be aware of his strength around her, to keep at least half of it in check. *Smaller than you.* His hands shook as they climbed her smooth thighs, pushing up the dress she'd been tempting him in all day.

"Once I get inside you, it won't be easy letting you out of this bed." He could barely make out his own voice; it had dropped so many octaves. But Christ, Samantha leaning back on her elbows, eyes like saucers, thighs quaking in his hands? Not every day a man encountered something so out-of-this-world gorgeous. "Right now? Yeah…" His chest hit the mattress, shaking it enough to send Samantha bounding up a few inches as his knees landed on the ground. "Right now, your pussy needs the tongue of a grateful man."

He surged forward, burying his open mouth against the swath of her panties, yanking her legs until they were bent around his head. An image of the pink sparkly underwear formed a devilish idea in his head, along with the compelling need to lick her naked pussy, and Duke tore the material with a quick twist. There she was, then, slick perfection waiting for his mouth to work magic on it. *God. Damn.* There were women. And then there was *Samantha.* The little bud he planned to make a meal out of peeked out, just a hint, reminding him of the woman herself. Inviting without realizing it and ripe for pleasure. *Christ*, he needed to rake his cock up and back against that flesh. Later. *Later.* Right now, he would taste her between the legs, before he made her too sore to appreciate it.

"Are you—" Her flat belly shuddered up and down. "Are you doing this all because I put on SportsCenter?"

"Not going to lie, that got me real fucking hot. Thinking about you in here, setting up a surprise for me, worrying whether or not I'd like it. Scooting that chair around, your ass twitching beneath your dress. Yeah...if you didn't already have my cock hard as marble, that would have done it. But it only added to what was already there." Duke trailed a thumb down the middle of her sex, moving slower on the incline, stopping just before the spot begging for touch. "Never thought about a woman's clit so much in my life. *Damn,* sweetheart. I've been...needing to *get* to it. My dick hurts for one single woman. And there's a little spot between her thighs that likes to be rubbed." His harsh groan vibrated the bed. "Couldn't sleep last night for thinking about your clit."

Samantha's fingers were doing their best to shred the comforter, and hell if that didn't make his balls draw up even tighter. At this rate he'd cross the finish line before she did, simply from watching, tasting, smelling her. "Your hands. Oh my God, I-I...your hands."

Judging her wet enough, Duke slipped his middle finger into her pussy. "What about them?"

"Ohhh." Her ass lifted off the bed, making Duke curse. "They're so rough. Like rocks. Or..."

Alarmed, Duke started to withdraw his finger, but it only made her moan. Loudly. Loud enough to be heard in the hallway, which he didn't mind a damn bit. "You *like* them rough."

"*Yes.*" Her enthusiasm made it a requirement for Duke to rest his head on the mattress a moment, gathering himself. *Tight, willing woman. All for me.* When he lifted his head again, Samantha wasted no time grabbing on, guiding him closer. "Please, Duke. Please?"

Oh shit, that display of neediness cut his tether. He went at her nasty, stiffening his upper lip and dragging it back and forth over her clit, his middle finger fucking her wetness nice and slow. Samantha wasn't shy about needing relief and he *loved* that. Loved the way she dropped her knees open, holding his head in place, loved the way she writhed and jerked every time his tongue flicked her pink bud. Sure as Duke was mouth fucking Samantha, she fucked him right back, meeting his licks with gentle rolls of her hips. This *woman*. She would match his voracious hunger in bed, and that certainty made his cock one jealous motherfucker. It strained behind his fly, hating Duke's mouth and fingers for having the privilege of sating her first. In an attempt to placate his angry flesh, Duke reached down and squeezed, rasping a growl when the situation only escalated, semen rising from his tip. A wet tease of release that represented only a fraction of what his balls were holding.

His mouth never ceased in its assault on Samantha's flesh, tongue joining his fingers in a few thrusts before slipping back to the bud he'd been craving.

When the spasms began in her legs, they cinched tight around his ears, Samantha's fingers clutching frantically at his head, his shoulders. And something wild and turbulent woke up in Duke's chest, a roar ripping through the jungle of his conscious. Without pausing to check his instincts, Duke reached up and took Samantha's jaw in an unforgiving hand, tilting her head back and gripping tight. Ownership. Over her body, her orgasm. His. *All of it.*

"Duke. Keep going just like that. *Ahhh.* Oh God, I'm—I'm—"

Samantha's thighs turned into a vise, her lower body wrenching up toward his mouth, trapped screams painting the air. Duke added his ring finger in the rhythmic milking of her pussy, pride flashing like blinding light behind his eyes as she came, and came, bucking and calling his name.

No sooner had the lightning passed and Duke heaved himself on top of Samantha, supporting himself on two massive forearms. He ground his erection into the juncture of her thighs, groaning over the heat that seeped through his fly. "I'm going to wear your come all night, sweetheart. Right where it's meant to be. On my cock, like a badge of fucking honor. I'm going to run my hand over it when no one's looking, feel that dampness and remember the sweet pussy it came from." He dropped down, giving her nowhere to look but his eyes, nothing to feel but his swollen johnson. "That's Duke's clit between your thighs, Samantha. No one touches that clit but Duke. You need it polished, teased, banged, or just plain slapped, who's the one you call?" Leaning all his weight to one elbow, he gripped her jaw once again. "Be a good girl when you answer and I'll kiss it again later."

She answered through a mouth swollen and dotted with teeth marks. "Duke. I call Duke."

He gave one final ferocious drive of his hips before rolling to the side. Seeing Samantha sweaty, flushed, and out of breath, dress rucked up around her waist, Duke couldn't subdue the urge to pound his chest. Twice. *That's how I handle what's mine. Just like that.*

Yeah, he heard himself. Or at least, the bristling beast living inside him, seemingly controlling his words and actions. Not only had he mentally referred to Samantha as his—the woman *and* her accompanying parts—he'd spoken them out loud. To her.

Duke didn't say things he didn't mean. Which begged the question: what now?

Jesus, he'd just formed a certified addiction to this woman. On top of liking her. A whole goddamn lot. So there would be some figuring out to do. Tonight. Because Samantha up and vamoosing back to Manhattan next week without plans to see him again? Over his lifeless corpse would that be happening.

Unyielding in his resolve, Duke scooped Samantha's pliant body off the bed and sat down in the chair she'd arranged for him, grunting over the way she tucked her head beneath his chin. Having her snug little ass on top of his dick wasn't exactly good for his sanity, but he'd meant what he said. If they got in bed now, they wouldn't get out until tomorrow.

"What about you?" she whispered, walking her fingers up his chest.

Duke caught her wrist, bringing it to his mouth for a kiss, battling a smile at the way her pulse ticked in overtime. "You'll be taking good care of me later."

"O-oh," she responded, on a hitched breath. "Presumptuous."

His smile won and he tugged Samantha closer, just as the half hour of glory known as SportsCenter kicked off once more. And they watched together.

Chapter Eight

Feeling buck naked while fully clothed was a new experience, indeed. Samantha rode the elevator down to the lobby beside Duke, her pulse applauding his earthy, male scent, his lack of dressy clothing. That vein that ran down the center of his bicep. The way he'd tucked his tongue into his cheek in lieu of saying hello in the hallway. The slightly wrinkled quality of his T-shirt and the fact that he probably didn't give two craps. All of him. Just a big man meal, leaned up against the elevator wall with his arms crossed, frowning. At her.

After Duke had oral sex'd Samantha half to death, she'd fallen asleep in his lap, only to be roused an hour later, mortified to learn she'd drooled on his chest. Yes, drooled. Was there an alternative outcome in an all out, post-orgasm unconsciousness? And not just *any* orgasm. *The. Orgasm.* The one women—including herself—chase with various battery-operated mechanisms after men fail to do the job well enough with their tongues.

Duke's tongue. Samantha tugged on the hem of her leather skirt, unable to believe how aroused she became at the memory. Should have worn jeans. The whisker-roughened flesh of her inner thighs felt on display, marking a path to *there*. Her loved-up nether regions. Everyone would know by looking at her she'd been participating in *something* of a clandestine nature. Heck, they'd figure it out by talking to her, since she'd screamed loud enough earlier to strain her vocal cords.

When Duke had left Samantha to shower, he'd stopped her from closing the adjoining door, conveying with a look that he wanted it kept open, before sauntering off to close himself in the other bathroom.

And that's when she realized...she liked that idea. Of having unfettered access to one another. Not because Duke could sneak in any time and finally take care of the erection he'd been sporting since entering her room. Not *only* that. Although it appealed quite fantastically.

Where was I?

Right. Being in what surmounted to the same room with Duke meant...she could talk to him. Benefit from the safe place he surrounded her with, just by being close. Yes, her attraction to Duke was out of control. Her knees were honest-to-God knocking as the elevator descended, along with her stomach. But, in a horrific twist, other feelings were pushing through the seams of her lust and...blooming.

His gruff, affectionate manner with his sisters, the way he'd housed his friends without question during hard times, the selfless qualities he seemed to play off, amounted to this big, wise, protective bear...that wasn't interested in a commitment. Little wonder, too, considering his entire life appeared to be one commitment after another. Work responsibilities, family obligations. Duties he completed, because to ignore them meant being untrue to his nature.

Granted, Samantha didn't want any romantic entanglements, either. They'd both been clear about that at the starting gate. It just…seemed an awful shame that someone so spectacular would spend his life alone. She thought back to the sketch she'd snuck onto paper in the steamy bathroom after her shower. A solo Duke dressed in winter gear, sticking a flag into a mountain peak, flying the words JUST ME with pride. Why did something she'd known about him since their first meeting form such a horrible pit in her stomach now?

Duke's big hand sliding over her leather-covered backside riffled Samantha back to the present. Her breath huffed out in a rush. "What are you doing?"

"Looked like you needed a distraction," Duke said in her ear, squeezing one of her cheeks with a relishing groan. "Or maybe I was just distracted by this. I can't tell."

Samantha couldn't help but arch her back, allowing Duke to look her over, top to bottom, which he did with a blistering perusal. "You want to get back to me?"

"I *want* to get you on your back." They were across the elevator in a tangled kiss before Samantha even noticed Duke making a move. Hands twining in her hair, he gave the interior of her mouth a long, room-spinning lick, nudging her against the wall with powerful hips. He rolled against her once, twice, before pulling back with a frustrated curse delivered at her forehead.

"Your ability to turn a phrase is impressive," she murmured, the lamest compliment of all time. Who was she? His English teacher?

The elevator doors rolled open on a lower floor, an older couple stepping on, hitting the button for casino level. Duke carried on as if they were still alone, however, speaking at his usual volume. "Need to talk to you."

"Go right ahead." Samantha grimaced. Plastered against Duke's He-Man body, every word out of her mouth sounded like porn dialogue. "I mean, go right *ahead*."

Face meet palm.

Duke didn't seem to notice she'd repeated herself, though, examining her ear as he tucked a length of her hair behind it, rubbing his lips together in a dangerously hypnotic move. "This thing with you and me, Sam…"

"What thing?" *There's no thing…is there?* She breathed, her pulse skipping like stones across a pond. Just as Duke opened his mouth to respond—*with what?*—the cell phone in her purse went off with Rhianna's "Bitch Better Have My Money," the ringtone she'd cheekily selected for her brother without considering she might find herself in public one day when it sounded. *Somebody shoot me.* Desperate to put a cap on the loud vulgarity that echoed in the elevator, which had earned her a reproving look from the older couple, Samantha dug through her purse and sent the call to voicemail.

When she deflated against the elevator floor with a sigh of relief, Duke looked anything but amused. No, he seemed to be pondering the merits of upending her bag and dumping the contents—including her phone—one the elevator floor.

"Who's calling you?"

"Renner." She frowned up at him. "And don't you dare say anything bad about him. He's a good man who's done a lot for me."

"Yeah?" He tipped Samantha's chin up with his forefinger. "So why aren't you taking his call?"

"Because."

Duke shook his head, sending a flush up Samantha's cheeks. Thankfully, the elevator door chose that moment to open and she made a dash toward the beckoning lobby, where people were spilling into the casino from several other elevators in the bank. River and Vaughn were supposed to meet them just inside the casino entrance, so she proceeded in that direction, only to be pulled to a stop by Duke. He guided her just outside the moving, animated crowd, continuing until her back met the wall.

Samantha smacked his hands away. "You're always... *situating* me."

"You didn't mind it upstairs, sweetheart."

"Oh, that's real nice," she huffed, smoothing the leather of her skirt, tugging down the hem, his nearness still making her feel nude. "When you remind someone about a favor, it steals the generosity right out of it."

His thumb tucked beneath the snap of her skirt, dragging the material down just a touch, circling his callused digit over her skin. "Woman like you lets me under her dress to get a lick and you think *I* was the generous one?" He half scoffed half grunted. "Getting drunk on your pussy was a favor to *me*, Samantha."

"You say very bad things," she breathed, barely bypassing a moan.

"Haven't even begun." His hand slid over to settle on her hip. A possessive move. "Talk to me about the phone call. About your brother. Or we ride the elevator back upstairs so I can work on getting it out of you another way."

At some point, she would reach her limit for this male chauvinist bull crap...but apparently it would take just a little longer. At least, according to her lady parts, which were feeling quite tolerant at the moment. "It's just Renner being Renner. He knows about the broken engagement and no doubt has an arsenal of ideas to change my mind." Samantha sighed. "He only wants what's best for me."

"And the ex-fiancé is what's best for you?" Duke growled, caging her with both powerful arms propped on the wall.

"No. He's not," she said patiently, feeling compelled to hold Duke's gaze for a few beats. "But Renner thinks differently than everyone else. He doesn't know how to express affection for family, so he situates them. A little like you, except he backs people into a corner with money in the name of caring. Including me."

Duke's voice dropped to a dangerous volume. "How's that?"

"We're going to be late—"

He stopped her warning with a slow melding of their mouths, his impatience clearly harnessed under the sensuality. His head tilted, lips opening wide in a devouring kiss, leaving her knees shaking when he pulled away. "Talk to me, Sam."

Holy God. Who had she become? That woman being kissed passionately in public, making everyone uncomfortable, that's who. So why did she want to climb him like a sequoia tree and beg for a replay? "He was going to co-sign on the bank loan for me. Renner, I mean." She dragged in oxygen. "For Art on Wheels. The money would be my startup capital to purchase the vehicles, the supplies, advertising, not to mention cut my hours *way* back at work to run the venture. He could have just *given* me the money, but I wanted to have responsibility. I wanted to be the one who paid the loan back."

"I understand that," Duke said. "I understand."

Those softly spoken words turned the lining of her belly from acid to caramel. "But his signature on the loan was contingent on me...marrying first." Discomfort moved in again at the reminder she'd broken a promise to someone. *Two* someones. She knew all about the damage severed trust could cause. How it could make you doubt every interaction. Doubt the sincerity of others so much you avoid human connection completely. "It wasn't an arranged marriage—I was free to choose my future husband—but I-I'd already accepted Hudson's proposal. The stipulation was just Renner's way of strengthening the business. *Everything* is business to him, but this time there was a purpose." She swallowed with difficulty. "It isn't always easy for Renner in this industry..."

"You mean, because he's gay."

"Yes," she answered. "I wasn't sure you knew."

"I knew. It just didn't have any bearing on my opinion of

him. Keep talking."

"I really like you," she breathed, knowing she sounded silly but physically incapable of blocking the words from leaving her mouth. Duke just kind of grunted, either as an acknowledgment or a signal for her to continue. She didn't know. "Hudson and I—" Another, more irritated grunt. "Uh…we were going to get past the doors Renner can't seem to get a foot through, but I'd still have time to run Art on Wheels. But I couldn't do it." She closed her eyes and blew out a breath. "I couldn't commit."

Duke's eyes were dark as he processed her words. "And now, the loan you were depending on…you're not going to get it. Even though that business is your dream." His expression turned to disbelief. "He can't hold you to that. This…*Hudson*…left for three years."

"My brother makes his own rules." His snort ruffled her hair. She tried to shrug, but the invisible weight on her shoulders wouldn't allow it. "The truth is if he'd only left for three *weeks*, I would have broken it off." She gave him a half smile. "Commitment-phobe, remember?"

"Huh? Yeah. Right." He didn't so much as crack a smile in return. "So this meeting on Monday…"

"I'm going to apologize. Because if I couldn't follow through, I never should have made him a promise. And I want him to see I mean it." She paused. "I'm going to ask Renner to co-sign the loan, anyway. I owe it to myself and the other artists to try one last time to make the business happen in the original time frame." Samantha swallowed. "It probably won't work and I'll have to gather the funds on my own, which could take…years. I'll probably just get an earful about responsibility and honor and feel even worse afterward." She threw her arms out to the side and executed finger-wiggling jazz hands. "*Family*."

His mouth remained in a grim line. "And on top of the

guilt trip you don't deserve, you think he'll try to convince you to give this prick another chance?"

She let him skate on the name calling. "Without a doubt."

"Well." Duke gave a firm nod and stepped back, making her miss his strength in an instant. "Let me be the first to say *fuck that.*"

He clasped Samantha's hand, storming toward the lobby, leaving her no choice but to jog along behind him, wondering what the hell he'd meant.

Chapter Nine

Duke could feel Samantha's questioning look as they—along with River and Vaughn—traversed the tunnel leading them to the VIP section of the Caesar's Palace concert hall.

Front row seats. Just his luck.

Also? Not happening. No one behind him would be able to see over his gigantic ass, so he'd spend the evening taking eye daggers in the back from the regular-sized people. As soon as he situated—yeah, he was owning the accusation—Samantha in a place he felt comfortable leaving her, he would wait outside. At least the time alone would give him room to think.

About how to convince a fellow commitment-phobe to marry him.

Tonight.

Funny enough, he hadn't broken out in hives yet. Not a panic attack or flashback to his childhood in sight. Maybe his nerves couldn't navigate their way through his sudden need to keep Samantha from that Monday meeting. Or to face it with her, side by side. That image was one he couldn't shake.

Him and Samantha, sitting down in front of Renner's big, fancy desk, holding hands. The intensity with which he ached thinking about it…hell, it was throwing him for a fucking loop.

Samantha loved her brother, not to mention owed him a debt for putting her through school. If anyone could convince Samantha to give her failed relationship another try, it would be Renner, whether out of exasperation or guilt, since broken promises seemed to be a serious issue for her. Well, that second try with another man would be happening when pigs flew on broomsticks through the Holland Tunnel.

Nope. Not on Duke's watch. Granted, marrying a woman—when he'd sworn to remain a bachelor for all time—was an extreme measure to take. But the opposing magnets in his stomach that cranked to full intensity every time Samantha was close by? They were in hyper force now. This ex-fiancé… *Hudson*…was back in town as of this week. Way too soon for Duke's comfort. Who knew what kind of a man it took to land Samantha as a wife. This guy could look like Captain fucking America for all Duke knew. Combined with Renner's efforts, Samantha could be taken out of Duke's reach, when he hadn't figured out what to do about her yet.

She liked him, right? Thought he was hot? She'd said so herself, while in a position where lying doesn't come easy. And upstairs in her room, she'd let him rip off her panties. Not something a woman allowed unless she at least held a passing admiration of the man doing the ripping. Shit, he needed to stop thinking of her spread legs or his dick would need its own concert ticket.

As they drew closer to the stadium entrance, he could feel the vibration of the crowd under his feet. Samantha walked along beside him, excitement making her face even brighter than usual, and Duke didn't bother checking the impulse to throw an arm around her shoulders. "You keep smiling like that, people will be watching you and not the band."

She ducked her head, swerving a little to deliver an elbow in his side. "Keep talking like that, I'll think you're trying to butter me up for something."

What? Like a proposal?

Christ, the girl busted a hole in his gut every time she looked his direction, and at the same time somehow patching up all the holes inflicted over the years. After watching so many marriages fail around him, he'd found it laughable when anyone decided to trust the institution. Well, hell if he wouldn't have a little sympathy next time some poor sap proposed on the factory floor to his lady. Apparently it was possible for a woman to burrow under your skin so deep you were afraid to see what happened if you yanked her out.

Not that Duke could let on she'd gotten to him. Big time. She was just as skeptical of relationships as he was—case in point, her broken engagement. So he'd have to play it right or watch the whole plan blow up in his face.

At the end of the tunnel an usher in a red jacket held a door open for them, scanning the barcodes on their tickets with a device hanging around his neck. "Best seats in the house," he said with a chuckle. "Enjoy yourselves."

"Thank you," River squealed, earning a kiss on the forehead from Vaughn.

Samantha was all but bouncing as they slid into the darkness of the venue, and even Duke had to admit, the atmosphere was a long way from Hook. Camera phone flashes went off from every seat, hands clapped in a rhythm, whistles pierced the air. It had been a while since he'd attended a concert, but there was no way to mistake the anticipation of the band about to emerge. Feet stomped, women shrieked... and then, there was Sarge Purcell, with his fiancé—Duke's ex-co-worker—Jasmine Taveras at his side. Their drummer and bass player, whose names Duke didn't know, took up the rear, waving to the audience.

Duke, Samantha, River, and Vaughn reached the front section—which was standing room only for approximately three dozen people—and Duke came to a stop, reluctantly urging Samantha to continue without him.

"Why aren't you coming?" she shouted over the noise.

"No one will be able to see over me," he ducked down to say against her ear. "Go on ahead. Just…be careful, sweetheart. I don't like all those people jumping around, knocking into each other." He tugged on a strand of her hair. "What ever happened to actual seats, huh?"

Samantha's expression when he straightened was a mixture of sympathy and…something else. She looked a little bit like she'd just watched one of those puppy videos on the internet, which made no damn sense whatsoever. He didn't have time to examine too closely, though, because Samantha took his hand and pulled him toward the rear of the VIP section, despite his attempts to stonewall. Duke knew a determined woman when he saw one, however, so he went along, appreciating the way her ass twitched back and forth under her leather skirt. How long was this damn concert going to last? If he didn't get a piece of Samantha soon, he would start bargaining with the Devil.

They reached the back of the VIP crowd and Samantha gave a brisk nod, wedging him back into the gated corner with busy hands. "There, Goliath. You're not blocking anyone here." She batted her eyelashes up at him. "How does it feel to be situated for once?"

Duke bit back a smile. "Go on up to the front. I'll keep an eye on you."

"Are you crazy?" The cords of the opening song began to play. "I'm not giving up the best view in the joint."

He stooped down to see the stage from Samantha's vantage point, giving her a skeptical look when bobbing heads blocked everything. And that was when Samantha slung a leg around his neck, seating herself on his shoulders. There was no way to hold the smile back after that. He gripped her ankles and rose to his full height, laughter rumbling in his chest when she squeaked. Laughter that cut off rather abruptly a moment later, when Samantha's pussy made its presence known at the back of his neck, her inner thighs warming his unshaved cheeks. Every once in a while, her tits would brush Duke's head, making him wish he was facing the other direction, putting him mouth level with her sweet spot. God, she'd tasted incredible earlier. Whatever girly lotion she'd applied to her legs smelled like sugar cookies, and his stomach rumbled, starved for one thing only. Samantha.

Aware that he was completely ignoring the concert and, frankly, not giving a rat's ass about the onstage entertainment one way or another, Duke traced his thumbs up the backs of Samantha's calves and felt her shiver. He continued on to her knees, remembering the way she'd cried out when he'd fingered her. *Your hands. Oh my God.* With his dick gobbling up real estate in his jeans, Duke rasped his palms over Samantha's knees and up her thighs, groaning when she writhed a little, rubbing her warm juncture against the back of his neck.

If they'd been alone, Duke would already have both of her sweet ass cheeks in his hands, face buried between her legs. Feasting. Unfortunately, they were only on the third song by the time Duke's mouth joined the mix, lips running along the curve of her knee, tongue licking the crease on the underside.

"Duke," Samantha moaned above him, her voice barely perceptible above the crowd's wail. "Let me down."

Knowing he would miss the feel of her thighs hugging his head, Duke nonetheless crouched forward, allowing Samantha's lithe body to slide down his back. He turned to find her looking dazed, so he took her arm, tucking her against

the front of his body, making goddamn sure her ass felt his
hard cock. Holding her there to suffer with him. Samantha
went up on her toes, tilting her head to one side, issuing a
clear invitation for Duke to kiss her neck.

Even though his mouth was watering in response, Duke
restrained himself, leaning down to her ear instead. "Need to
talk to you."

"Again?"

"That's right," Duke grumbled, not at all happy with the
complaint in her voice. He'd thought their conversations were
pretty damn enjoyable, but maybe he'd been wrong. That
didn't bode well for their marriage. "I've been sorting some
things out."

Samantha tilted her head back to meet his gaze, a little
smile tilting the corners of her sexy mouth. "Like laundry?"

"No." Already the discussion wasn't going as planned.
"I've decided we should get married."

Of course, the loud guitar solo chose that moment to drop
into a quiet strum, leaving the words *we should get married*
hanging in the air, drawing the attention of everyone standing
in front of them. Duke frowned until they went back to
minding their own business, and by that time, Samantha had
turned around with a face full of *what the fuck*. "Married?"
She sputtered. "Are you drunk?"

"No, but I'm considering it," Duke muttered, before
raising his voice to be heard over the once-again raging guitar.
"Can we talk about this outside?"

Samantha hesitated a moment before nodding, winding
her way through the pulsing crowd, leaving Duke to follow
in her wake. It took them only half a minute to reach the exit
door and walk out into the hallway, which was empty, save the
usher who'd scanned their tickets. Neither of them seemed to
mind the audience, however, because they launched right in
where they'd left off.

"Please tell me you were joking," Samantha said.

All right. The stab of hurt Duke experienced at her words was just ridiculous. "You think I would joke about shackling myself to a woman?"

"No," she hedged. "I don't. So what gives?"

"I'm getting there." Duke scrubbed at the back of his neck, hating that it felt so hot. "This agreement with Renner, it only says you need to be married, right? Doesn't name this...*Hudson*...as the only one who fulfills the terms?"

Samantha nodded slowly. "That's right."

"Well." He advanced on her, pleased when she stayed put. "I don't know anything about the kind of man it takes to land you, Sam, but I, uh..." Damn, he'd rather get electrocuted than list his good qualities. "I served my time overseas. And there's no one who knows the factory like me. You can do a lot better, but I was kind of thinking you could do worse, too. Than me." He took a few seconds to corral his thoughts, wondering if he had the metal to say what came next. When he didn't think he could back it up. But he would've said anything in that moment to put a claim on her, wrong or right. "And it'll work because neither of us wants a...traditional marriage. No pressure or expectations, like you might have had with the other guy. We would know the score going in." He tried to read Samantha's mind and couldn't. "This way, you'll get to start your business—"

"And Renner gets the outward appearance he needs in the boardroom. Right, I get that." She looked perplexed, but Duke thought he might have glimpsed a ray of hope, too. "What do you get out of it, though? You're not doing this for an interest in the company..."

"No," he said firmly. "I'll sign it all away."

"Oh," she breathed. "Back to my original question, then. What do you get out of marrying me?"

Duke had always been honest to the core so the half

truths he'd told were eating away at his gut. No more. "I may not want a wife, Sam. But I sure as shit don't want you as someone else's wife, either." *Wow.* That sounded way worse coming out of his mouth than it had in his head. He felt a little like socking himself in the face. "This could be more of an…arrangement, if you want to call it that." More words that sounded wrong. Really fucking wrong. Samantha *deserved* a real marriage and he was offering her a sham. Still, when a man wanted something this bad, he couldn't just let it slip away. "But I'd like to see you beyond this weekend. When we both agree to make it happen."

Her eyebrows went up. "So…you're marrying me so I can be your occasional hookup?"

"No." Although, that was what his offer had amounted to, wasn't it? *Jesus.* "I want you for more than that."

"Such as…"

"Barbeques. Watching you draw." He thought of her mooning over the egg sandwich and peeking over the top of her sketchpad. "Watching you do anything, really."

Color appeared on her cheeks. "That sounds relationshippy."

"We can call it a friendship, if you want," he said, judging she was about ready to veto the idea and ready to pull out all the stops. "So long as you don't just skedaddle back to Manhattan and forget about Duke."

"Okay, you have to stop referring to yourself in the third person." Her cute, bubbly laugh filled the hallway. "Also, *skedaddle*?"

He crossed his arms.

Samantha shook her head. "Aren't you worried about Renner's reaction?"

I'm more worried about you being out of my reach. "Your brother might have upgraded the facilities and equipment, but that place doesn't run without me. If he's not smart enough to know that, I don't want to work for him, anyway."

A series of beats passed where she seemed to be judging his sincerity. "I can't let you do this, Duke." She reached out and laid a hand on his arm, genuine feeling lighting her eyes. "Much as I appreciate your selfless sacrifice to lock down no-strings sex…" She shrugged. "I know you're just a rescuer guy. You see a woman in need of help and you can't stop yourself from trying to fix it."

Duke snorted, disbelief clogging his filter. "Sweetheart, I might want to solve your problem. But you're solving mine, too." He uncrossed his arms to take her chin, tilt it up. "And my problem is you being available."

"It wouldn't matter." She sounded impatient. "I'm not getting back together with Hudson. I don't even *know* him anymore."

His throat burned just hearing her say the other man's name. "He's not the only man out there. And I'm not taking any chances."

"You can sleep with me without being my husband." Her eyes darted to the wall behind him. "We can even be exclusive…for a while…if you want."

Duke's touch tightened on her chin without a command from his brain. "I *do* want." He bent down to lay a wet, searching kiss on her mouth. "I *need*."

Samantha's breath bathed his lips in a rush. "This is insane." She tugged her chin free and paced away, Duke's eyes following her, body poised to chase her down if she bolted. And why wouldn't she? He'd made a royal mess out of the whole conversation, asking her to be his legally-bound booty call, for chrissakes. When she returned, the toes of her high heels nudged the tips of Duke's boots, turning something over in his chest. "I really don't like putting one over on my brother. I don't. And I wouldn't, either…" She blew out a breath. "… if I didn't think he'd just respect me for being strategic, like him. Honestly, it would serve him right for making marriage a condition in the first place."

Duke tried to squash the hope, but it prospered, anyway. "Is that a yes?"

"Not yet."

Why did she seem suddenly nervous? "Spit it out, Sam."

"*God*, this is a proposal for the books." Her hand fluttered near her throat. "I just…commitments are tricky, aren't they? People are always breaking them."

There it was again. Another hint that Samantha's phobia of relationships had originated in a different place than his. What had she been through? Right now might be the wrong time to ask, but he *would* be finding out. "I won't break this commitment to you, unless you ask me to do it. That's my word."

At that, she stopped fidgeting. "Are you sure about this?"

"*Yes*," Duke answered without hesitation.

More pacing. "What do you call a melon that can't get married?"

A fine time for jokes. Sweat was rolling down his back, heart beating in his throat. And through it all, he wanted to hear the punchline. "I don't know. What *do* you call a melon that can't get married?"

"A can't elope."

Duke smiled at Samantha. Samantha smiled back.

She stared at him so long, with such gravity, he stopped breathing. "Okay, Duke. You have a deal."

Chapter Ten

There weren't many times in Samantha's life she could remember feeling instantaneously changed. In the past, teachers, parents, and co-workers had asked if she felt any different after a milestone birthday or post-graduation. And not wanting to disappoint them, she'd occasionally lied and said yes. *I feel older. I feel freer.* Maybe those changes had kicked in later and she'd just never stopped to acknowledge them, but tonight, having married a man she'd known such a short time, the difference in her emotional makeup was a tangible thing.

Mostly because she was terrified she'd made a mistake.

Not because she didn't like Duke. No, her fear stemmed from liking him *too* much. Giving him too much power to break her when their duty to one another ended. And it *would* end. Obligations always expired, no matter if they took one day or three years. Or if they occurred legally or mentally, with one party checking out, losing interest. Yeah. Tonight, she'd set herself up for a fall.

So why had she done it?

To help Renner's company by becoming a stable figure in the boardroom? Yes, that had helped her decision to marry Duke along. A lot. When she'd broken her engagement, she'd broken an agreement to help the man who'd done so much for her. Marrying a good man with a decorated military background—Duke—would repair the trust she'd broken. But there was more.

A little seed had been sewn last night when Duke kissed her in the building vestibule. The ownership in his eyes, the way he'd touched her…there must have been a small, long-denied piece of Samantha that *craved* the chance to belong to someone, as sure as they belonged to her. But something told her no one could have tugged that reaction out of her…but Duke. When she'd been adopted by Renner's father as a pre-teen, there'd been a sense of completion and security. One that had eventually been torn straight down the middle. She'd never wanted to risk such a catastrophe again. Had something shifted? Something that might convince her to take a chance?

The recklessness of such an idea simmered in her blood as they walked into her hotel room, Duke shutting the door with a definitive *click*.

It was too late to be cautious, as evidenced by the certificate in her purse. But when Duke began to close in on Samantha, her mind chanted one eager phrase. *Bring on the fallout.*

And there was that look again from Duke. Probably the way Adam had looked at Eve, or more accurately, the way a caveman had looked at his first source of food. *Mine.* He didn't even have to say the word; she could feel him thinking it. It starved her. Even knowing she would pile her insecurities back on in the morning, tonight she *wanted* to be preyed upon. Wanted to sink into that possessiveness Duke projected and revel in it. Because she'd never experienced it before. Never once.

Duke reached behind his head, grasping his T-shirt at the neck and yanking it off in one fell swoop. "What are you thinking about?"

Mother Mary. There were men. And then there was Duke Crawford. He wasn't pretty or sculpted. Didn't have the kind of physique that would land him on the pages of a calendar or on a "hot bodies" board on Pinterest. No no. Duke was husky and covered in hair. A bear among mere cubs. His muscles were slabs she wouldn't be able to lift if they were separated into individual muscle packs. *Muscle packs? You're losing it.*

"I'm thinking about dismemberment," Samantha whispered.

Duke cocked an eyebrow. "Come again?"

"Y-you know. Cutting you up." *Oh my God.* She'd gone full Dahmer. "That came out really, embarrassingly wrong. I was just thinking your…parts…look so heavy, I probably would need a wheelbarrow to carry them. For the purposes of transport." She was actually someone else's horror story. Live and in the flesh. "You're beautiful, i-is the bottom line. You're huge and angry looking. Like maybe you could wrestle the Yeti and win. Even your slight beer belly is doing funny things…to me. I should have stopped at dismemberment, huh?"

When he threw a thoughtful glance down—presumably at his belly—mouth moving into a grim line, Samantha almost went into a full swoon. It was as though his appearance had only recently occurred to him as semi-important and that lack of vanity basically lit a Bunsen burner beneath her ovaries.

"It's my turn to ask what you're thinking about," Samantha said, shifting on the plush carpet.

His big paw came up, scratching right in the center of his chest hair. "I was thinking I could switch to light beer for you."

"Romance, thy name is Duke."

He sauntered closer, head titled to one side. "I'm not sure

you want to know what I'm really thinking about, sweetheart."

Duke's chest. An inch from her mouth. Coarse, masculine hair brushed her lips. "It can't be any better than what I'm thinking."

"Which is?"

"Why hasn't he taken his pants off?"

"Romance, thy name is Samantha." Their laughs were low and simultaneous. Samantha couldn't stop herself from leaning across that final breath of space to press her lips against his chest, feeling the rumble. Duke's hand slid into the back of her hair, twisting, drawing her away. "I'm going to tell you something. You listening?"

Samantha nodded, heat swarming in her stomach over the deeper timbre of his voice. "Yes."

"Good." His grip tightened in her hair. "It's my wife's job to take off my pants. You want what's on the other side? Get your hands to work and unzip my fly."

Her short breaths echoed in her head. *I've been claimed.* His rough touch and matching words might have appalled Samantha, coming from anyone else, but Duke's delivery of them made blood whiz to her head. Perhaps because he'd given her such pleasure earlier, taking nothing in return. Or maybe he'd simply tapped into a need for submission she'd never been aware of. "Own me," she whispered, closing her eyes, dropping her fingers to his zipper, tugging down. "Direct me."

"Mean what you say, Sam." Duke's mouth pressed to Samantha's forehead, releasing a prolonged growl. "*Mean it.* So I can be as fucking demanding as I feel."

She pushed the loosened pants down his hips, smoothing her hands over his brawny, flexing buttocks on the way back up. His hard flesh bobbed between their bodies, primed and ready, Duke's hot breath pelting the part of her hair. God, she wanted to be manhandled, commanded by this giant enforcer.

Maybe she had the moment they'd locked eyes across the bar. Had everything been leading here? To this moment when a previously unknown need would be slaked? "I mean it."

Duke bared his teeth at her temple a moment, then she was being led—by the hair—toward the small dining area. Even as she stumbled, excitement surged like a geyser, dampening the walls of her insides with fevered lust. Samantha didn't catch sight of Duke's fully naked body until he dropped into a chair, guiding her down, down, until both knees hit the floor. His thighs were horizontal monuments on either side of her head, just as solid and crude as the rest of him, that insistent hand still delivering pleasure-pain to her scalp.

"What else does a wife do for her man?" His tone was a chisel bashing into stone. "Show me with your mouth."

Her breath arrested at the sight of his arousal, full and ruddy. A prominent vein running the full length. Shiny at the head. Much like his appearance, Samantha imagined he didn't give much thought to his manhood, either, except to release stress, maybe in the mornings before hiding it away in work pants. It would remain there all day, stowed between powerful thighs as he worked. Like a man. With his hands. Greased up and grunting. And all the while, his male flesh grew heavier in his underwear, building up steam for the following morning.

"Samantha, get out of your head," Duke gritted out. "Before your silence gets into mine."

"How could *you* be worried?" she breathed.

No sooner had the question escaped in a rush, did Duke grip his intimidating erection, his fingers tangling in her hair, almost clumsily. "You...see things like an artist. I'm far from a work of art."

Her heart swelled so rapidly, she went lightheaded. "No. You're much better."

Skepticism met with relief on his face. Perspiration had formed on his chest already, his stomach lifting and diving on severe male shudders.

Actions, not words, were needed here. She was awed by Duke's mixture of power and gentleness. Him thinking anything less wouldn't work for her. Samantha's lips parted without hesitation when met with the wet head, the flesh made even larger by his tight grip at the base.

"Can I have your suck, Sam?" Duke rasped. "I'm dying for your suck."

Samantha could sense him trying to be easy, pushing himself into her mouth. But the sheer size of him and the abundance of his need didn't allow for tenderness. The hand he'd encircled himself with shook, falling away to land with a loud slap on his thigh when she gave him that first long pull. She swirled her tongue around his big tip, glorying in his moisture, his choked groan.

Duke's huge hips thrust to meet her mouth halfway. "I don't expect you to take it down your throat, sweetheart. Okay? Just…just stroke me off. Work in as much as you can. I'm so hot just knowing your mouth is making the top of my cock wet." As if his body wanted to prove the claim, the round head swelled in her mouth. "Can you taste how bad it hurts from being around my little wife? From licking her pussy and wanting to cram itself inside?"

Samantha's eyes glazed over, a furious beat beginning between her legs. She slid her thighs open farther on the carpet, moaning as the leather skirt slipped up, bunching around her hips. Gripping her like two hands. Her hips tilted back like Duke was already behind her, getting ready to consummate their marriage. Every erogenous part of her body was clamoring for sex. For Duke. For *force.*

"Yeah, I see what you want down there." His thundering growl shook her insides. It was desperate, hot, hungry. She could actually hear his aggression trying to take over and she gloried in that loss of control. *Making* him lose it. "I see that

slick body getting in position to take my cock." His head fell
back on a deep moan. "I won't be able to stop with the tip
when I get between your legs, sweetheart. I'm sorry. Every
inch of me is married to *every inch* of you. I need to show you
what that feels like. I need to show *myself*."

Duke's promises were made with such conviction, she
whimpered around his pulsing flesh, so scared to allow that
possession but unable to deny her eagerness. With Duke.
Only Duke. And with his voiced intention to have all of her,
Samantha's instinct to please overrode everything else. With
a deep breath through her nose, Samantha loosened her jaw
and sunk down, purring when Duke nudged her throat, those
mighty thighs shaking on either side of her head.

"Ohhhhh, *fuck*. Fuck. Can't believe…can't believe you
did that." Before Samantha could release Duke from her
mouth, she was hauled to her feet, giving her no choice but
to balance herself by planting both hands on his shoulders,
leaning down to bring them face to face. "God help me, I want
to hear you say I'm the first one back there. All the way back
where you swallow. Say it."

"First one," she managed, feeling her eyelids sag. Between
her thighs, neediness became an urgent problem. Oh God, he
was turning from gentle giant to beast, snarling against her
mouth, his arousal lying like an invitation across his abdomen.
"Look at you," she whispered. "Some kind of warrior or—"

"If you're going to talk, Sam, do it naked."

Was she still wearing clothes? Puzzled, she looked down
to find herself still fully dressed, although her neon pink
panties were on full display beneath the hiked up skirt. She
pushed off Duke's shoulders to a standing position between
his splayed thighs and moved her hips in a figure eight.
"Undressing me is my husband's job."

He moved so fast, Samantha jerked under the sudden
attack of hands. He lifted the clinging tank top over her

head, raking two callused palms down her breasts, whispering prayers she couldn't discern, before unclasping her bra in front and then flinging it backward. Getting the leather skirt off required Samantha to aid him by wiggling, making her breasts jiggle and, right before her eyes, Duke's erection lifted and strained against his stomach. Removing his touch on a curse, he began to stroke himself, rough, rough, teeth gritted, sweat pouring down the sides of his face.

Look at how I affect this formidable man. If she pushed him just a touch more, would he dominate her again? Was he doing it now *without* any physical contact? Felt like it. Every cell in her body was compelled, driven to appease this man's lust, and the need for a connection she felt burning under his surface. Even though it scared her, there was a frayed wire dancing around in her middle, needing to plug into his almost visible loose end.

Energy crackling along her skin, Samantha shimmied out of her panties and straddled Duke's massive thighs, letting their mouths hover a breath apart. "Now…where was I, husband?"

• • •

If Samantha hadn't just called him by the title he'd been craving, her ankles would be pressed down over her head on the bed about now. Come was already dribbling down the sides of his cock, his stomach and balls so tight it was a wonder he hadn't lost consciousness yet. This woman, this tight little phenomenon with a sex-kitten voice was his wife? Jesus *Christ.* She was going to be the death of him.

As if she hadn't already done the impossible and deep-throated him, she'd demanded in that sassy voice that he strip her naked, that show of mettle making him hotter than sin. And now? Now her pussy was pressed down on his come-soaked dick, tits sliding through his chest hair, that mouth a lick away from French kissing. "If you need slow to be satisfied, I'm going to need some time to calm the hell down." His stomach muscles constricted painfully. "*Christ.* You've got me so fucking amped. I need to know up front how rough that body of yours can take."

Her uneven breath drifted over his lips. "Why don't you find out for yourself?"

Good question. One he had the answer to, even though it made no sense in his state of agony. He shouldn't be prolonging this period of hell before their bodies were finally locked together. "Damn if I don't want to hear what you were going to say, Sam. About you seeing me as some kind of... warrior. So just get to saying it."

A little sound eked out of her, blue eyes widening a fraction, before her voice drifted out, sounding like rumpled sheets. "When I was on my knees, you reminded me of a battle warrior, sitting here, getting his due." Her smooth thighs slipped higher, closer, on his sweating legs, stopping at his hips. Sliding back again. "I pictured you riding through town and picking a girl in the adoring crowd. For your guards to bring back to the castle. To service you."

His cock stiffened that final notch into misery at the picture her words painted. Samantha being escorted into his room, left with the duty of sucking him to an orgasm. Riding him to one. Being available the next morning to take his morning wood between her thighs. "And you're that girl. You...like being that girl."

Samantha nodded. "With you, I do."

Possessiveness burned behind his eyes, painting everything around him in grit. "Good answer." All night, he'd been dying to get his hands on Samantha's bare ass cheeks and he wasted no time now, palming them, squeezing them until she winced and sobbed. His roughness turned her nipples into little pink points. *My match. She's my fucking match.* And any remaining doubt Duke was harboring over Samantha being turned off by his aggression vanished, making way for the final tumult of lust. "Bend back and grab my jeans."

Fog rolled into her gaze, tongue skating over her full bottom lip, all in the mere second before she did as he asked, performing a back bend in his lap to retrieve the pants. *Christ almighty.* With her tits pointed at the ceiling, her thighs flexing where they draped over his own, pink panties stretching over her pussy, this woman he'd married was something out of a jack-off dream. The kind where a man woke up and was forced to change his shorts. Only about a million percent hotter.

She returned to her original position with the jeans, taking the condom out of his front pocket without having to be told. Then she dropped his pants, ripped open the condom with her teeth and stretched the latex down his girth. All with a dutiful, lip-biting, wide-eyed expression that put a stranglehold on his balls.

"Goddamn, you're something else," he rasped. "I'm going to be beating down your door in Manhattan the first night you spend away from me. You realize that, don't you? Wanting my wife. Needing her little body under mine." The heat behind his eyes grew more intense, his pulse whipping into frenzy. "Now I'm just thinking of you in bed without me. So on top of being the horniest I've been in my life, now I'm desperate. You're breaking me and I haven't even been inside you yet." He took hold of the pink fabric between her legs and turned the panties into a useless rag with a twisting jerk of his fist. "Climb onto my cock, Samantha, and dance for me. I'm trying really fucking hard to make sure we don't consummate this marriage with your face pressed into the floor."

By the time he finished speaking, her breath was labored and shallow. The hand she placed on his shoulder shook, the opposite one taking hold of his erection, making Duke roar

a curse up at the ceiling. "My warrior wants me to dance..."
Her whisper was issued on a shudder. "And I want to please
him."

Heat—snug and sweet—slipped down on his hard
flesh in one fell swoop, through her obvious lack of recent
experience, leaving both Duke and Samantha groaning
against one another's mouths. Trading disjointed words and
licking kisses. Duke's lungs started to ache and he realized he
wasn't breathing. Not breathing. Not moving. Barely able to
comprehend the raging bursts of light playing on the backs of
his eyelids. Greenery bloomed across his scorched earth, the
sensation of her surrounding him so breathtaking, he came
back to life with a throat-razing gasp.

"*Samantha.*"

"*Duke.*" Her head fell to one side, eyes so tightly shut
her forehead was puckered. Ten fingernails burrowed in the
flesh of his shoulders, her slight body vibrating on his lap. "I
kind of...*wow*. I kind of jumped into the deep end here," she
murmured. "It's...I haven't in forever...and *you.*" She moved
her hips and set Duke off roaring. "Holy... Is this thing
registered as a weapon?"

Duke buried a hand in Samantha's hair, dragging her
mouth up against his own. The pain in his stomach demanded
he jerk her hips up and back to find relief, but the bleary
quality of her gaze reached into his chest and twisted. *Want
Samantha here with me.* And Samantha's reality relied on
being a dreamer, so he latched onto that, needing to drag her
back to the insanely high plane she'd left him on. "Is that how
you speak to your warrior?"

Her pupils bled into the blue of her eyes as they focused
on him. "S-sorry." She slid her hips back on his thighs and
writhed forward, puffy lips falling open on a feminine moan.
"Oh my *God.*"

Knowing it would take every ounce of concentration not

to climax too soon, Duke leaned back in the chair, throwing both hands behind his head to grip the wood. And Christ above, from there, he could watch his length slip in and out of her pussy, those final few inches taking an extra effort to find their home. Something about his new position got Samantha going big time, her hands raking down his heaving chest, the tempo of her hips increasing until her ass slapped down on his thighs. *Slap slap slap.*

"Is that better?" she choked out, dragging her nails across his nipples. "Does this please you, warrior?"

Fuck. Fuck. Was this woman—this phenomenon—really bound to him legally? Yes. *Mine.* His hold on the back of the chair was so tight his fingers ached with the effort. Allowing one hand to drop away, he let it ride on her bucking ass. "Faster. *Please,*" he grunted. "When I'm all the way in and you give me that extra little press down...fuck, that's so good, sweetheart. If it doesn't hurt too much, grind down...*grind. Yes.*"

Samantha whimpered, biting her lip as she followed his instructions. "Stop worrying about h-hurting me...you f-feel *amazing.*"

"That right?" Duke almost roared, turned on to an incredible degree. "So I don't have to worry about you pouting all day tomorrow, because that big cock you're riding made your pussy hurt?"

"No." She shuddered on top of him. "Maybe."

Needing her mouth, Duke surged forward, capturing her eager lips in a panting, slippery kiss. "If it does hurt in the morning, I'll find somewhere private to cup you in my hand. Right where it's sore. I'll apologize and give you a nice, easy rub. Kiss the sexy mouth that took me to the throat."

Just the idea of soothing his sex-hungover wife intoxicated him, made him want to slap a fist against his chest. "Your going to have no doubt how much I appreciate being allowed to squeeze myself into your body. If I ever think you're unsure, my tongue will service you between the legs until there's no question. Until you scream the doubt free, along with my name."

She fell forward onto his chest with a sob, the pumps of her body kicking up to a wild speed. They were meshed together, sweaty flesh to sweaty flesh, and still Duke yanked her closer. *MINE.* He might have shouted the word, because she clung to him as her pussy took in his dick, again and again, as if she wanted to climb inside his body. Live there. And he would have welcomed it, because it would mean no one but him would be able to have her. Or see her. Or touch her. "*Duke.*" She spoke in a strangled tone at his ear. "More. *More.*"

Again, instinct guided Duke, his fingers tracing up the slice of her bottom, where he pressed down on her back entrance with two fingers. "Ah, Sam. If me touching you here makes you come, you're going to meet the beast. You understand me?"

She was already moaning when his ring finger dipped, just a touch, into that forbidden passage, and her entire body jerked, her pussy wrapping so tight around his dick, his teeth drew blood biting down on his upper lip. He was no longer himself after that. Or maybe he'd *always* been this man, but no woman had ever tapped into the bruising power under his surface. Samantha did. Samantha. Samantha.

It took the effort equivalent to fifty oxen, but he waited until the gorgeous dream with the tight-fitting pussy—*my wife, my fucking* wife—on his lap stopped trembling, before standing and taking three strides to the bed. Samantha's back landed on the mattress, brown hair spreading out like a victory flag while Duke settled between her legs and began a frenzied pumping, hot breath puffing out through his nose like a bull. There was no finesse in the way Duke finished himself off.

And hell if she didn't encourage him with urgent hands and fervent screams of his name. And yeses, so many of them, he lost count.

"*Yes, yes, yes.*"

He went down on Samantha's body, shoving his face into the crook of her neck, yanking her legs up around his waist. "Go ahead and say no," he growled at her ear. "Go ahead and try it."

Only a beat passed before she dug her heels into his ass, as if attempting to dislodge him, that slick body bucking beneath him. "N-no."

Duke bore down, driving into her with twice the force, sending the headboard bashing against the wall, snarling into her neck, the sound of his slapping balls echoing in the room. "Who's a good little wife, huh? Who's a tight, wet wife?" He snapped his teeth down on her neck then sucked the flesh, making a mark. His mark. Pounding began on the room's back wall, voices shouting…even the phone started to ring, and still he drove his cock into his heaven on earth, glorying in the way she yanked him by the ass into the cradle of her thighs. *Fucking* right, *that's my woman.* "Go on, sweetheart." Duke slid a hand down between their drenched bodies, stroking her clit. "Tell them my name. Loud enough for them to remember it and tell the stories to their friends at breakfast. About the girl in the next room getting it so hard, they had to call security. They'll have no idea I'm the one who worships you. That I would work overtime for a decade just to hear you call me a warrior." He buried his lips in her hair. "*Go on.* Confuse them. Say my name loud enough that they think you're going to open your legs for it whenever I unzip my jeans. But we both know I'll be begging you to let *me* unzip *yours*. You might be the loud one, but I'm your pussy slave."

"Duke. *Duke.*" Samantha came again, her body contorting beneath him, mouth opening to release a throaty cry. Tears slipped down her temples, which would have alarmed him if her expression wasn't pure ecstasy. If her lips weren't skating up and down his flexed bicep, her tongue licking out to capture his salt. And that's what sent come shooting up the thick stalk of his dick, into the warmth of Samantha's body. After everything, it was the affection. The way her mouth curved with happiness as he shook and growled, chest heaving, perspiration dripping, on top of her spent form. It was the affection that made one fact inescapable.

He was completely *lost* for this woman.

And she was already his wife.

Duke collapsed on Samantha with a smile, knowing there wasn't a damn thing that could change that fact. Not without his consent. As in, not happening.

As he moved to his side and crushed a pliant Samantha into a bear hug, both of them already drowsy, a niggle of premonition skated up the back of Duke's neck, but he ignored it in favor of watching Samantha sigh against his chest. In favor of holding his wife on their wedding night.

Chapter Eleven

Samantha was not a morning person. At age ten, she'd been sent to sleep away camp while her mother was getting acquainted with her second husband. One morning she'd slept through her six o'clock alarm—even managing to sleep through an hour of rambunctious young girls getting dressed—making it necessary for the counselor to rouse her awake. At which point, Samantha had clocked her. And it had taken *a good hour* for regret to set in. That was before she'd become a coffee drinker. With the introduction of caffeine, the rage window had been narrowed down to twenty-five minutes, which she considered a remarkable improvement.

Duke's masculine scent on the sheets had Samantha's eyes flying open then squinting back down in protest of the sunlight. The reality of morning reached into her skull like serrated finger bones, jostling her skull until she started groaning into her pillow. She tested her limbs on the crisp linens and stopped abruptly. Oh. Oh...*wow*. Back to back kickboxing classes couldn't have accomplished this level of soreness in her thighs. Nope. Only a merciless factory mechanic with enough bulk to create a Samantha outline in the mattress.

God, even her calf muscles were aching. How? Straining through the three most intense orgasms known to womankind? Yeah, that was *probably* responsible. Another wiggle on the bed revealed a throb in her abdomen, between her legs.

That last realization sent a thrill racing head to toe, sensitizing every inch of her naked skin making contact with the sheets. Last night had been…whoa. *Seriously* whoa. Waking up with someone else in the room wasn't a typical Sunday morning. In fact, she couldn't even remember the last time she'd shared a bed overnight with *anyone*. Even her physical relationship with Hudson had been pretty wham-bam-thank-you-sir, always followed by Samantha zooming back to her own apartment. But falling asleep in Duke's unyielding grip hadn't required a moment of thought. She'd just done it. Because it had felt…like a destination. Not a pit stop.

I'm married. I'm married to Duke. Panic fluttered up into her throat. He wasn't in bed now. Had he left? Relax. She needed to relax. They weren't…this wasn't *emotional*. Just an arrangement, right? A high-pitched noise started in her right ear, forcing her face farther into the pillow—

But it cut off abruptly when Duke chuckled. "Damn, sweetheart. I'd hate to see you hungover."

Relief tried to rush in, but it only managed to fill a third of the holes. They'd sprung up too quickly to catch them all. "You don't want to talk to me before coffee."

A white mug clinked down on the bedside table. "I didn't know how you took it, but I figured on black."

She pushed up on one elbow, hair tangling over her eyes. "Are you calling me bitter?"

"No." He pinched the sheet draped over Samantha's back, lifting it for a completely unapologetic peep show. "I'm saying if you get any sweeter, I won't get a minute's rest. Worrying about everyone who wants a taste."

"You're a jealous man."

"Yeah. I am." Duke's baritone threw a shudder down Samantha's back, but she stilled when his hand molded to her backside, kneading in an unhurried, possessive rhythm. His callused palm scraped up her spine, his touch clamping around her neck. Holding while she sucked in shallow breaths, staring at the pillow but mentally painting his face. Harsh, intense. "I'm jealous of last night's Duke, because this morning's Duke hasn't had you yet."

"Well…" Lust wrapped around her middle. "That's a n-new one."

He grunted, using his thumb to massage her nape. "You sore where I've been?"

Such an intimate question and yet, in the sheets where they'd slept wrapped around one another's bodies, it somehow seemed like information they would share without question. "Yes."

A gusty sigh left him, his hand leaving her neck. "About how long is it going to take you to wake up?" He cleared his throat. "I've got a thing out here. On the balcony."

Wishing she were still being petted, and rather annoyed by that realization, Samantha sat up and took the steaming mug, inhaling deeply and sipping. "What thing?" She grumbled into the mug. "I don't do things in the morning."

She peeked through her hair to find Duke rubbing his chin, looking more than a little uncertain. "It's nothing."

"If you're talking about anything, it's something."

The lines between his eyebrows eased. "You been paying attention to me, sweetheart?"

"Yeah." Her stomach felt like it was being pumped full of helium. "You're pretty hard to miss."

"Good."

With that, he lumbered off toward the balcony, his limp more pronounced than usual. Because of last night? Samantha took another cobweb-clearing swig of coffee and stood, frowning at the universe in general. Or maybe just because his leg hurt, but he'd still put together a *thing*. Where did he get off, looking good *and* being thoughtful first thing in the morning?

Duke's T-shirt from the night before still lay on the floor, so she snatched it up, attempting to pull it over her head without setting down the coffee. And when that didn't work out, she set down the mug to try again, snickering when the shirt reached her knees. After giving her teeth a quick brush in the bathroom, she reclaimed her coffee and slogged out onto the balcony.

The scene that greeted Samantha made her suck in a breath. On a reclining deck chair, in a big patch of sunshine, Duke had set out a tray of egg sandwiches—more than she could ever eat—a giant coffee urn, and her sketchpad. All on top of the bed's big, puffy comforter, which she must have been too tired to notice was missing. It was a sun-drenched drawing haven, overlooking the Atlantic City boardwalk. "This is the thing?"

"I told you it wasn't a big deal," Duke said, taking up half the outdoor area with his mass. "Just repayment for the uninterrupted SportsCenter." He waved a hand at the deck chair. "So do your thing."

Was this the same man who'd growled *who's a tight, wet wife* last night? Samantha was so dumbstruck, Duke almost managed to breeze past her back into the hotel room. "Wait." She looked down to find she'd grabbed his arm. Or a tiny portion of the muscular appendage, more like. "I can't eat all this on my own."

"I had four already."

"Geez." She searched for another way to keep him on

the balcony, because…why? Normally she couldn't tolerate human beings until she'd showered and drank two cups of coffee. But with the sun beating on her back and Duke's body warming her front, she could do nothing but acknowledge that Duke's heat won by a landslide. "Can I draw you again?"

Surprise crossed his features, but he nodded, leaning back against the wall. Crossing his brawny arms. "I thought you might want to be alone."

Samantha backed up until she could sit on the deck chair, placing the sketchpad on her lap. "Why?"

His profile was so strong, so breathtaking, as he stared out at the Atlantic. "I got to thinking maybe I was a little hard on you last night." He flicked her a look. "Just because we have something unconventional here, doesn't mean you should be…handled like that on your wedding night."

Without a command from her brain, Samantha's hand started to move across the paper. Not as fluid as usual, though, because her pulse was ricocheting all over the place. "So this is more apology than repayment?"

Watching her beneath hooded eyelids, Duke gave a stern nod. "Call it whatever you want, Sam. I just don't want you to think you made a mistake. Saying yes to our…arrangement."

The panic she'd convinced to recede upon waking drew back in slowly, like a tide on the shore. She was feeling too much here but couldn't seem to get a handle on the undercurrents Duke set sailing so far below her surface. *Arrangement.* Why was she having such a difficult time remembering what was really going on between her and Duke? Clearly, he didn't have the same problem.

She needed to keep her head on straight, eyes to the front. Neither one of them had hidden their fear of commitment since meeting at The Third Shift. If she let herself believe Duke's possessive attitude went further than a—albeit heavy— sexual attraction, she would be in for a serious fall.

The kind she'd protected herself from since youth. He didn't want her sleeping with anyone else. So what? That didn't mean he'd be clearing out a sock drawer for her things or…putting an actual ring on her finger to symbolize their conditional marriage.

"What's going on over there?"

Duke's gruff question shattered the ice of her thoughts. She stared down at the picture she'd drawn, while barely being conscious of her hand's movements, and waved Duke over. Eyes narrowed, he pushed off the wall and came toward her, laughing when he saw the result. On the white space, a comically barrel chested Duke was depicted as a mustachioed Casanova, a rose clamped between his teeth.

Samantha shielded her eyes from the sun to look up at Duke. "Thanks for the thing." She picked up an egg sandwich and took a bite. "I love the thing." Forcing her tone to stay light, she tugged on his pant leg. "I loved last night, too. Um. A lot."

. . .

For the first time since waking that morning, Duke took a satisfying inhale, filling his deprived lungs to capacity. She'd loved last night. A lot. He was ignoring the *um*, because for some crazy reason, Samantha was blushing, looking nervous. Which was just laughable, considering he would have heaved himself over the balcony if she'd said otherwise.

As soon as he'd gained consciousness, Samantha's soft body beside him, he'd started replaying the best sex of his life. No—*best* sex didn't do last night justice. That phrase left the possibility that he'd ever experienced anything close. Or even *imagined* anything remotely as fucking satisfying as giving that final pump into Samantha's tight, eager body and coming while she moaned his name. His cock ached with the sense memory, his balls drawing low in his pants. Getting heavier. Needing his woman.

She's sore. She's sore because you mauled her like a lion on steroids. If he didn't want to screw up this situation with Samantha, he needed to play it slightly cooler. Not try to drag her back into the sack before she'd even finished her breakfast.

Unfortunately, playing it cool didn't help him figure out why Samantha suddenly wasn't looking at him—something he *really* didn't like—so he nudged her chin up. Something sharp turned in his chest. How could there be shadows in her eyes with the sun shining directly on her face? "If there's something wrong, I need you to tell me."

"There's nothing wrong," she laughed.

"Sweetheart, I have four sisters. When nothing is wrong, the world is on fire."

She waved off his concern. "I think I'll just draw for a little while." When she gathered her legs up toward her chest, allowing the oversized T-shirt to slide down and reveal bare, sun-warmed thighs, the situation in his pants grew dire. "Join me?"

"That chair isn't big enough for me by myself, let alone both of us."

She stood up, straddling the piece of furniture, her gaze dipping to his fly. "I think we can manage if I'm on your lap."

Duke had no idea where the new slap of intuition came from. But he suddenly knew, without a doubt, Samantha was avoiding. And her weapon of choice was sex. Not a good thing, when he didn't have a single tool in his own arsenal to combat the sweet relief Samantha could provide. Or even a way to restrain himself from giving *her* pleasure, because— Christ—that privilege couldn't be neglected. He craved it like a scuba diver with no oxygen tank craved the surface.

You created this situation. You based the whole

relationship…hell, the marriage…on sex. Fix it.

He swallowed the golf ball in his throat. "Sam, you're wearing my shirt…and you already smell like me underneath it." He fingered the material of the shirt she wore, letting it fall back against her waist. "I know that because I rolled you over in bed and smelled your skin—your belly, tits, and thighs—to make sure. You've got me on you, head to toe. But you're already aching from last night's fuck. And if I sit down in that chair, you're going to get me up inside you again, too. There's no help for it."

Slowly, she lifted the shirt over her hips, letting him see her bare ass looking taut and fresh in the sunlight. "Don't I know it, honey?"

Duke's groan probably woke people ten floors above. "You're playing dirty calling me honey."

"You like that?" she whispered. "Honey?"

God, if it weren't for the hint of distance in her expression, he already would have been doing his damndest to break the chair, Samantha impaled on his erection. But the touches of stress around her mouth told him to slow down. Her attention kept flickering away, as if there was a whole different ball game taking place in her head and it was bottom of the goddamn ninth.

Duke garnered his will then slipped in behind Samantha, sitting down with her on his lap. And yeah, he was well on his way to death. *Death.* Especially when Samantha assumed they were getting started, giving her buns a hot tweak, up and back on the ridge of his cock. Misery dropped down on his shoulders like thousand-pound weights, but he wrapped his forearm around her waist—stilling the seductive lap dance—and bit down hard on his bottom lip.

"Show me what else you've got in that pad," Duke rasped.

Samantha stiffened. "Why?"

That was the million-dollar question, wasn't it? He'd

married Samantha so no one else would take her away. Right? Or had he just been fooling himself? Here he was, ready to beg for the whole damn package. All of her, all the time. Unfortunately, he'd set himself up to be allowed only half the stars in the Samantha galaxy. It was possible she didn't *want* to talk with him about anything important. They were husband and wife...with benefits. *Only* benefits. Well that was going to change, because more than just an attraction had been formed the night they'd met, but he'd based everything on it, like a thick-skulled asshole.

So here was the jump. The leap. And he was taking it with eyes wide open. He wanted to date his wife, bat shit crazy as *that* sounded. So he would take it slow and pray Samantha followed. Already her body was ready to snap in half in his arms, probably in shock that he'd put the brakes on sex.

"What?" he mumbled into her neck. "I can't possibly be interested in art because I'm a machinery mechanic?"

Samantha's lips were pursed in an *O* when she turned. "Of course not. I would never think that—" She cut herself off upon catching his wink, set the pad down, and reached for her coffee. "No fair, I'm a half step behind in the mornings."

Duke plucked the coffee out of her hands and set it down beneath the chair. "Art now. Coffee later."

"Stealing someone's coffee is called mugging," she whined.

"Ah, if you can pun, sweetheart, you're wide awake."

"I can pun in my sleep."

Duke nudged her head with his chin. "You know, drinking too much coffee can cause a latte problems."

Her gasp of pleasure was almost worth his cock being tortured, because she twisted in his lap, those lips open like a prize. "Nailed it."

"Yeah?"

"Yeah," she breathed.

For a space of time, their attention remained locked on one another, making Duke's ribcage feel too tight. He couldn't stop himself from leaning in and planting a soft kiss on the corner of her mouth before moving to the opposite side and doing the same. Must have been too much or too revealing, because before he got enough of her sweetness, Samantha spun back around, throwing the book open and leaving Duke feeling starved. For eye contact, for her breath. Everything. "Art," she croaked. "Not that puns aren't art, but…"

"I get you." He tucked hair behind her ear. "Show me."

She tilted her head to the left, giving Duke a view of her neck. The sound of pages flipping, the call of a gull, along with the muffled roar of the ocean and Samantha's humming… all of it worked together to calm something in him. Odd, considering he'd always thought himself a low key man. But nothing compared to the peace that stole over him with this woman on his lap. It was bone deep, and it shifted past and future until they formed an arrow pointing right at them, where they sat on the balcony.

"This one…" Samantha murmured, urging Duke to sit forward and look over her shoulder. "This one is from a third-grader. I volunteered at his school in the Bronx over the winter, while I was doing some trial runs for the business." She held up the depiction of a small boy soaring over the Manhattan skyline, each of his hands holding on to an even younger child, although the print appeared to be a copy. "Those are his brothers. He said if he had one wish—that was the day's theme—that he would take them flying. I think he meant in an airplane, but this made him laugh. It's one of my favorites. And ooh, there's this one…"

Duke dropped his chin down onto Samantha's shoulder as she rooted through the book full of sketches, finally pulling one out with a giant green dragon at the center. On the beast's back, a little girl performed a skateboard trick, flipping up in the air and gripping the board's edge. "Dragon skate park. This is my other favorite." Samantha turned a little in his lap, but Duke was so damn sucked in by her enthusiasm, he forgot to be annoyed over the multiplying ache in his groin. "She wants to be a professional skateboarder, but she'd never gotten the courage to ride outside of her backyard. A couple months after I drew this for her, she emailed me with a picture of her at a competition. She had a dragon on her helmet."

"You gave her the courage for that," Duke said, pride hitting him square in the throat. He wanted to bask in it but didn't know how yet. Or if she would allow it. "Art on Wheels," he prompted gruffly. "Tell me what that will look like when you get it...rolling."

"Oh my gosh, your jokes this morning are stellar." Her shoulders trembled a little with laughter. "There would be a universal routine, among each division of Art on Wheels. We would set up stations—five or six, depending on class size—and the kids would rotate. There would be a draw your story station. One where kids could create their own temporary tattoos, another to work on a mural. We would institute new ideas every month to keep it fresh. Anything that...breathes life, you know?"

"Normally, no, I wouldn't. But hearing you talking about it?" He shifted in an attempt to get comfortable. Didn't happen. "Yeah, I know what you mean, sweetheart."

She gave him a long, scrutinizing look over her shoulder before turning back to her pad. After a small hesitation, she tugged another drawing out from the pocket insert. Duke looked over her shoulder to find another sketch of himself. In this one he was hunched forward, the world resting on his back. "What about you, Duke? What do you want?"

His Adam's apple grew seven sizes. "What do you mean?"

"I think you pretend not to want all this responsibility—your sisters, the babysitting, your job—but maybe you secretly need it." She dropped the drawing and fell back against his chest with a sigh. "You claim to be a commitment-phobe, but you're just a big imposter, aren't you? Even to yourself."

She had to feel it. Had to feel the organ in his chest pumping in overtime. A denial of what he was only beginning to realize himself would be met with skepticism. Or worse, a pun. "What if I am? An...imposter."

The moment felt so stark, as if he could watch the seconds ticking by. But everything sped up when Samantha rested her hands on his inner thighs, trailing them higher. "I don't want to be another responsibility to you." Her hands found his fly and made fast work of freeing his desperate cock. He could no more stop Samantha from sliding back onto his lap, her bare ass cradling him, than he could prevent time from moving forward. She tossed her head back onto his shoulder, making eye contact. "Let me be the place you lose yourself instead."

No. His mind shouted the denial, but his body refused to hear. Lose himself? Deep in his bones was a vibration, making him wonder if he'd been lost *until* now. Until her. He wrestled with the need to growl how he felt into Samantha's marked-up neck, to make her understand his craving had carved itself far deeper than physical attraction, but her grip sliding around his erection turned up the roar of lust, drowning out logic.

And it drowned even further when Samantha's cell phone went off inside the room, loud enough to be heard over the Atlantic.

Chapter Twelve

Bitch better have my money.

She really needed to switch up her ringtone.

Behind her on the chair, she could feel Duke's mass coiling tight, as if ready to implode and rain earthy hotness down on Atlantic City. Apparently their quicky marriage the night before hadn't put any of his concerns to rest, regarding her brother and tomorrow's meeting. And even though there was a painful throbbing between her legs, one that tickled up into her belly, she nursed a hint of relief over the phone call's timing.

What if I am. An...imposter? What had he meant by that? If the flutter of nerves were to be trusted, Duke was trying to—what? Be *more*? She couldn't tell. Didn't know if he was just nursing the apology he'd issued for being rough last night. Or if...he wanted their arrangement to be something they hadn't discussed at the outset. And what worried her— *terrified* her, really—was the hope flickering like a lighthouse beacon right before her eyes.

She'd pegged him night one. He was a fixer. A caretaker.

That's all this was. And she couldn't let him muscle in and assert himself as *her* repair man. Or anything else for that matter. It was all well and good to call him husband and play house in bed, but this sweet side of Duke tempting her to sink down and get cozy…it couldn't happen. It *wouldn't* happen. Because she'd experienced a false sense of security and had the rug, the floor—hell, the whole foundation—pulled out too many times. Not again.

Last night, he'd been honest. As honest as the bruising, hot flesh she stroked in her fist. He was possessive of her body. And she would hold him to that. Hold both of them to that initial agreement. Anything beyond it would lead to a crash and burn.

"Go answer the phone."

Brought up short by Duke's command, Samantha stopped moving her hand and attempted to get her breathing under control. "What? Why?"

"Because I want your brother to know you're walking into his office tomorrow with a husband." He placed a hand over Samantha's, using their tandem grip to squeeze his erection. "I don't play games and that's what we're doing by ignoring the calls. Answer it."

There was a flush of warmth in Samantha's chest at his use of the word *we*, but she tamped it down. "I want to tell him about you in person. If we give him too much time to prepare—"

"Samantha." She turned her head just in time to catch a flicker of indecision cross his harsh features. "If you're ashamed about marrying one of his employees…a factory worker—"

"*No*." Denial slugged Samantha in the jaw. She released him and sprung to her feet, turning to place both hands on his broad shoulders. "Oh, you don't really think that, do you?"

Duke searched her eyes and seemed satisfied with what

he found. "No. I don't." His eyes ran down her body, pupils dilating, but the phone went off again. Beneath her hands, his muscles stiffened. "One of us is going to answer it. I don't think you want it to be me."

Swallowing a king-sized lump, Samantha walked backward into the dim, air-conditioned room, attempting to mentally prepare for the first verbal conversation with Renner since she'd broken her engagement. Broken their agreement. Taking a long breath, she snatched the dancing cell phone off her side table and slid a finger across the screen to answer. "Hey, Renner."

"Oh, you're alive. That's a plus."

Her lips curved in a wry smile, but it dialed down when Duke entered the room, his manhood still stiff, bobbing with each step in her direction, a look of intention on his face. "I-I'm alive. Am I going to stay that way?"

"I guess that depends." When the pause ran too long, Samantha closed her eyes, knowing that was Renner's way of building suspense. *Such a drama king.* "Did your trip to Atlantic City get the rebellion out of your system?"

Samantha's eyelids drew up as she rewound the previous evening. Had she posted on Facebook or otherwise given away her location on social media? No. She'd been pretty darn occupied by the hulking man who was now circling behind her. Slowly. "How do you know where I am?"

Renner's sigh was impatient. "Hook is a far cry from Manhattan. People talk here. They give a shit what everyone else is doing." A beat passed. "Five minutes in that dive that passes for a drinking establishment and I knew who you'd left with on Friday night." Duke's hands settled on her hips, attempting to steal her focus, but she held fast. "A quick visit to Mr. Crawford's house allowed his sisters to fill in the blanks."

"You didn't have to go to so much trouble."

"Well there's no one else to worry about you, Samantha. Is there?" Renner cursed in her ear, just as Duke applied pressure to the center of her back, pushing her upper body down to the bed, lifting the T-shirt up to her hips. "I didn't mean that the way it sounded. I just meant we're family and we look out for one another's interests. And it's in your interest to get back to Hook this afternoon."

Concentration was beginning to grow extremely difficult. Renner's reminder that she was alone in the world should have made her chest feel hollow. Should have hurt. But Duke's work-roughened hand sliding up her spine, the other kneading her bottom…they became the center of her universe. And when he shoved two fingers into her womanhood, forcing her to muffle a cry on the mattress, a thick drench of lust descended to banish any form of doubt. "I do have someone to worry for me," she murmured into the phone. "I worry for him, too."

A dragged out silence ensued, broken only by a foil packet being ripped open. "I assume he's there with you now."

Not a question. "Yes."

Duke's hand crept over her mouth, holding tight, and then he plunged his hard inches into Samantha, straight to the hilt, forming bright color blocks in front of her eyes. *Oh God, oh God, oh God. This is wrong.* There was pain because of Duke's size and her vulnerable position, but pleasure singed the edges just enough. Just enough. "Samantha." Her brother's voice was low and dangerous in her ear. "I hope you didn't do anything ill advised."

A slapping thrust from Duke made her eyes water, her mouth forming a silent scream. "It…" She trailed off to take a vital draw of air. "It w-wasn't ill advised."

"*What* wasn't?"

Samantha clamped her lips together to keep herself from calling Duke's name. She couldn't answer Renner. Couldn't focus on the words. Only shocks of pleasure-pain existed, Duke's big body ramming against her backside, propelling her forward on the bed, only to be dragged back.

"Get back to Hook this afternoon, Samantha. We need to—we *will*—straighten everything out."

"Fine," she forced out through trembling lips. "We'll be there."

There was a low growl from Duke, which forced Samantha to drop the phone, using frantic fingers to end the call.

"Oh my God." She bunched up the comforter and screamed into the soft material. "Slow down. *Oh my God…* please. It's too much."

Duke buried himself deep and ceased his drives, but the stretching sensation remained, making her light headed. "I don't like other men telling my Samantha what to do. Don't like them speaking to her like that. Talking to her *at all*." She barely registered Duke was referring to *her* in third person now, because his heaving bulk, his rasping breath demanded all her attention. He felt so large everywhere. Behind her, inside her. Even his hands encompassed her rib cage, before sliding down to jerk her hips up and back. "What do you mean *too much*?"

A broken laugh fell from her lips. Seriously? Everything about that moment defined those very words. And worse… worse, her heart was sprinting, a sense of fulfillment running laps around her chest. She loved his possessiveness. His almost beast-like claim over her body, her voice. If their situation was reversed, she would feel the same. Unbelievable but true. *No one tells my man what to do.*

One of Duke's hands tangled in her hair, a warning that went along with his tone of voice. "Answer me, sweetheart."

"Just take it slower…I'm still—" She cut herself off when a throb of need shook through her middle. Right where Duke's tip was located. "This feels different from last night.

You're deeper…touching me everywhere."

"That sounds like the opposite of a problem."

He gave a crude twist of his hips that had Samantha seeing triple. "Oh please. *Please*. I'm going to break apart. I can't break apart when I feel like this."

The T-shirt was torn over her head, thrown onto the floor, a split second before his damp chest smacked down onto her back. "Feel like what?" Duke ground out into her ear. "*Talk* to me, Samantha. I've got you."

Somehow she believed him. "I feel like…" Her thighs started to shake almost violently, along with her stomach. God, he wasn't even thrusting. It was just *Duke*, his giant presence, forcing his way into every inch of her consciousness. "I feel like if I…break apart, I'll be put back together differently. I don't know."

"What if I let you put me back together differently, too?" His tongue licked up and down the side of her neck. "What if I can't help turning into something new, don't *want* to help it…and need to see what Duke and Samantha look like when they change together? What then?"

Change? She couldn't. Didn't know how, right? But there was a definite shift happening that she had no clue how to vocalize. "I don't know yet. I…maybe I can't help it, either."

"Good. All right, wife. That's enough for now." Blunt fingers found her clit, rubbing in wicked circles, that title making her throat constrict. "There won't be any breaking apart happening this morning. I won't let my Samantha do anything she isn't ready for." He exhaled in her ear. "Even the word 'break' in the same sentence with your name makes me worry, sweetheart, but I'm addicted to this little pussy. I need to have it. So we might have to come close. Just enough to get a taste of breaking. Okay?"

His ownership and care for her coasted over Samantha like smoke. "Yes, Duke."

"That's my girl." His upper body increased its pressure, sinking Samantha down into the bed clothes, while their lower halves remained elevated. "You've got my balls jacked up so tight, I only need about ten good pumps. Are you close to giving me your come, too?"

"Really, really close," she whispered, wincing as her muscles contracted around his fullness. "Please, Duke."

She heard Duke's teeth clamp together on the first drive. His hips reared back and ground forward, his groan increasing in volume the deeper he reached. "Fuck, you have no idea how hot it feels sinking in. Starts off tight around my tip and clenches the more I push. Like maybe your pussy is having second thoughts...but there's no room for them because, *God*, it's so tight." Another prolonged filling of her core, complete with a rough hip tweak. "I need to remember to give it to you slow at first, though, don't I? It's the selfishness that makes me need to drill you so hard, sweetheart. You make me fucking crazy. I just want to *own* it. Selfish for *Samantha*." Hot breath spilled over her back. "But owning you only means something if you own me back. Without a single damn doubt. You understand me?"

His words jabbed at her mind, trying to break her from the lust hypnosis, but even when the gravity managed to penetrate...she found herself longing to hear those words repeated. Longing for them to be true. "Show me," she gasped, her belly beginning to dip and clench with the oncoming climax. "Make me feel it."

That was all the encouragement Duke needed, apparently, because he wrapped a meaty arm beneath Samantha's hips to keep her stationary, then proceeded to deliver one bruising pump after another, his balls making a loud spanking sound that whipped into a continuous burr of noise as his pace went into overdrive, his shouted curses vile and desperate. "You feel how *mine* you are?" His forearm jerked her into the blur of his thrusts. "That's how you're going to...*stay*..." A choked noise painted the air. "Let that pussy know it's Duke's property now. Squeeze me tight, sweetheart. Squeeze what's dying to belong to you and say that's what you want."

"*I want it, want you—*" Samantha cut herself off on a scream as the atmosphere broke into little pieces around her, oxygen burning in her throat, her lungs. *Worth it.* Worth it because of the twisting beneath her belly button, the blinding relief stealing through her middle, spreading to her limbs. The intense sensations seized Samantha as Duke released with an almost violent drive into her body, hoarsely chanting her name, before dropping down, pushing them both into the mattress.

"You want me, you have me." Duke jostled her prone form as he lifted up, dropping kisses along her shoulders and neck. "You have *us.* And thank God we straightened that out, so I can think with a clear head."

He wasn't laughing, either, as he rolled them over, tucking Samantha into his body like a kid does with their favorite blanket. Fear would rush in any moment, wouldn't it? She'd felt the stirrings of her least favorite emotion out on the balcony, but it seemed slow to respond now...

No. There it was. It crept in quietly as Duke began to snore into her hair. Her apprehension wasn't nearly as strong as usual. More like a distant thump of foreboding. She turned her face against his bicep, sucking in a breath when he pulled her closer. Maybe she could learn to live with the fear, just to have the incredible moments in between. It was better than full-on avoidance, wasn't it?

Samantha ignored the needles jabbing into her gut and let herself drift.

Chapter Thirteen

Duke really didn't like having Samantha out of his sight. She'd been quiet on the ride back from Atlantic City, buried mostly in her sketchpad in their shared back seat. To be fair, since they'd agreed to keep the marriage between the two of them for now, making small talk with River and Vaughn would have felt phony, which wasn't his or Samantha's style. Keeping anything from his friends for too long wouldn't work for him, either, though, so he needed him and Samantha on the same page.

When she'd asked Vaughn to drop her back at Renner's apartment so she could collect her belongings before the meeting, Duke almost had an aneurism. But he could see progress happening between them, could feel Samantha watching him thoughtfully, when she probably assumed he didn't notice. Yeah, he'd become dead set on making more of their relationship—too put it mildly—before Samantha got on board. Since his sanity seemed to depend on her following suit, behaving like a jealous, possessive caveman—outside of bed, as well as in—wouldn't help his cause.

Although, that description couldn't have been more accurate, could it?

He'd felt responsibility for people in the past. His fellow soldiers, co-workers. Definitely his family. But he'd never been...scared as hell they wouldn't need him back. And hell, he'd never felt fragile a day in his goddamn life, but put Samantha anywhere near him and he *swore* she could shatter him apart with a well-placed exhale. This relationship business was fucked up, but he didn't even want to consider what havoc *not* having a relationship with Samantha would wreak on his mind.

The way they'd bonded had been fast. God knew it had been. His instincts had woken up the moment she stepped into The Third Shift, though, and denying them was impossible, even if he still worried about his ability to be a better man. Better than the ones that had come before him. His sisters' husbands, his own father...what set him apart from those dickheads? Not a damn thing, far as he could tell. Had they all felt this scorching need to rearrange the puzzle of themselves? To fit the woman in and make her extra comfortable? He didn't know. There was no one around to ask, either. Vaughn didn't count, because what Duke's friend had with River was an anomaly. A one off. No way that brand of magic could happen twice, especially so close together.

What he did know for sure? Samantha needed to hurry up and meet him where he stood outside the factory, trying really hard not to be a caveman.

Just as he resolved to walk the eight blocks to her apartment, she rounded the corner, duffel bag slung over her shoulder. She paused a little on the sidewalk upon spotting him then continued his direction with a slight smile playing around her mouth. "Geez. It only took me half an hour to forget how huge you are."

As soon as she got within reaching distance, he lifted a

hand to cradle her jaw. "You didn't have to spend that half hour without me."

A shock of satisfaction plowed into his sternum when she nuzzled her cheek into his touch. "I needed to get my thoughts together."

He swallowed the panic. She wouldn't be nuzzling if she'd changed her mind about their situation. Which was only an "arrangement" for now, if he had anything to do with it. "You good now?"

"Yeah." She reached down and twined their fingers together, bringing them to her mouth for a gentle kiss that sent Duke's heart sputtering. "I think I'm good."

He forced himself to trust her answer as he led them to the factory entrance, lifting an eyebrow when Milo Bautista—a member of Vaughn's security team—stepped into their path, wearing his crisp navy blue uniform. Bautista had been in the same Army division as Duke and Vaughn, landing in Boston after his tour, his dry sense of humor already making him a factory favorite. Rumor had it, he'd played bodyguard to a famous pop star before landing in Hook for a fresh start, but Duke had yet to confirm. "Bautista." Duke nodded. "What are you doing here on a Sunday?"

The guy cleared his throat, suddenly appearing self-conscious. "I was on call." He split a hand gesture between Duke and Samantha. "Any time we have visitors, security needs to be on site."

"Visitors." Duke's jaw went hard at being called a visitor in the place he'd worked almost a decade. He glanced down at Samantha. "That your brother's way of setting the tone?"

"This is my unsurprised look," she answered with a smirk, but Duke could see her nerves already starting to pop, the color leaching from her face. "Could you please let my brother know we're here?"

Bautista turned on a heel without answering, using his

jangling set of keys to open the new steel front door, the
wrenching noise making Samantha jump. They followed the
security guard through the dark factory floor, their footsteps
echoing, before climbing the grated staircase to the offices,
one part of the factory Duke had never been to. He tried not
to dwell on that. How it proved the divide between employer
and employee ran deep in this town. They stood hand in hand
as Bautista rapped on the red office door, then he stepped
back to cross his tattooed arms.

Brisk steps sounded in the closed room—one, two,
three—before it sprung open, revealing the factory owner.
A suited Renner Bastion looked pretty much how Duke
pictured the devil. Too cagey and smooth to make anyone
remotely comfortable in his presence. Which—Duke noticed
vaguely—appeared to go double for Bautista, who went stock
still at Renner's appearance, a tick beginning in his cheek.

But when silence reined too long, however, Bautista
visibly shook himself. "Well, here they are, boss man." His
Boston accent echoed in the empty hallway. "Will that be all?"

Renner gave the security guard a blatant once over and
shrugged. "For now."

There were some pretty heavy undercurrents running
between Renner and Milo, but it made little difference to
Duke at that moment. Samantha's brother could very well try
to stand between him and Samantha—that's all he cared about.

Letting go of Samantha's hand so she could hug her
brother took a concerted effort. Even Duke knew that surge
of jealousy was ridiculous, but it was something he couldn't
get a handle on. It scorched like heartburn until she stepped
back, brushing Duke's side. Renner eyed him a moment—
the way a boxer sizes up his opponent in the ring—before
extending his hand for a shake.

"I suspect congratulations are in order."

Duke forced his grip to remain firm, but not crushing, as

they shook. "You suspect right."

Renner's expression was bland, but the confirmation Duke and Samantha were now married created tension around his mouth. "Well. That's one way to move up in the ranks, I guess."

Oh, this meeting was going test his willpower like a son-of-a-bitch, wasn't it? Instead of plowing his fist into the boss's smug face, Duke retained his cool. "Happy right where I am, actually. Loafers aren't really my thing."

"What *is* your thing?"

"Samantha."

Renner snorted while backing toward his desk. He dropped into a high-backed leather chair and gestured for Duke and Samantha to take the seats facing him. Duke released her hand in favor of smoothing it down her back, guiding her forward. As soon as they sat down, Duke dragged her chair closer, not satisfied until her knees bumped his thigh. And all the while, Renner watched them like a hawk. *Look your fill, man, and get used to it.*

"Samantha," Renner started. "We had an agreement, you and I. This company needed someone at the helm with a strong foundation in order to move forward. Do you have suggestion as to how I should proceed, now that you've broken your word?"

Duke felt Samantha flinch at Renner's word choice and had to bite back a growl. Not for the first time, he wondered about Samantha's hang-up about broken commitments and berated himself for not getting to the bottom of it. Had he used his time with her wisely? Goddammit, they'd had so few opportunities to figure out what made each other tick. He'd only begun to break through the invisible outer shell she wore, even though she'd made quick work of shattering his.

"I didn't break my word. Our agreement stated in order to take my place on the board of this company and have your help in securing funding for Art on Wheels, I needed to be married."

"To Hudson."

"No." Samantha's thumb brushed over Duke's knuckles and he forced himself to relax. "His name is nowhere in the agreement."

"It was heavily implied," Renner returned succinctly. "I guess there's no honor among siblings anymore."

Samantha made a miserable sound. "Renner—"

"You're less than enamored with relationships, so I always knew there was a chance you'd balk. I'd planned for that possibility." He narrowed his attention on Duke. "But I never expected you to trade one for another. What is it about Mr. Crawford that made the difference?"

He counted Samantha's breaths. One. Two. Three. "We're married, but it's not traditional in every sense. We—"

Renner's laugh cut her off. "Does Mr. Crawford know that?"

This was it. Duke was going to answer with the truth. He couldn't keep it chained inside. But Samantha's nervous glance in his direction made him hesitate, allowing Renner time to put up a hand.

"Never mind. That's a messy line of questioning." Leaning back in his chair, her brother crossed an ankle over the opposite knee. "I've always considered you my sister, even when our parents split. You definitely had no problem benefitting from that retained connection."

"*Enough.*" Duke's command went off like a bomb. "What's done is done. If you want to guilt trip someone, guilt trip the asshole who left her alone for three years."

"Yes. To oversee the lucrative investments that have made him a very rich man." Renner's lips curved into a smile when an extended silence followed his statement. Almost like he could see the crack running down the middle of Duke's body.

"Hudson is a Princeton graduate and a successful businessman. He's returning to New York as we speak to open his own firm, *in addition* to being a vital member of this organization." Renner shuffled through some of the papers on his desk. "What is your position again at my company, Mr. Crawford?"

"You know I'm a mechanic, so cut the bullshit."

Renner's laughter was dark. "You chose well, Samantha." He divided a look between them. "That was sarcasm, just to be clear."

Duke didn't want to acknowledge the gash of uncertainty that split through his armor. Samantha had been engaged to a probable millionaire who'd graduated from an Ivy League college. A man who could have given her anything. A home that *wasn't* filled with four crazy sisters. Vacations outside of New Jersey. Hell, a *ring.* What had he given Samantha since they'd met, apart from egg sandwiches and a sore body?

Fuck this. Duke straightened in his chair, laying a hand on Samantha's knee. He wasn't going to let this asshole get to him. He'd give Samantha what she needed. Soon as she agreed to be his wife in every way. They'd be happy. He wouldn't rest for a second until there was zero doubt of her contentment.

As if Renner could read Duke's thoughts, he steepled his fingers, regarding Duke from across the desk. *Searching for a new tactic.* Samantha beat her brother to the punch, however, speaking in a calm tone. "Renner, don't you *dare* try and insult Duke. He's a decorated veteran. He knows this factory better than you or I or Hudson. You have no idea how hard he works or what his day looks like. A man doesn't have to be a investor to—"

"I'll sign the loan for Art on Wheels, Samantha," Renner cut in, brisk and impatient. "You want the money for your business, it's yours." He rolled open his desk drawer and removed a file. "All you have to do is sign the annulment papers, ending your marriage to Mr. Crawford."

Chapter Fourteen

Samantha morphed into an ice sculpture. She could see herself sitting on top of a buffet at some fancy wedding as everyone moved past, far more interested in the shrimp cocktail. Duke must have frozen solid, too, because his hand was blistering cold where it lay on top of her leg. *All right.* She'd known something like this was coming from Renner. He never failed to catch everyone around him off guard.

If she signed the annulment paperwork, she'd have her business. Everything she'd been dreaming about. And… having her business funded was the reason she'd married Duke in the first place. Wasn't it? She'd assumed they would have an argument on their hands in dissecting the contract— and proving Hudson wasn't the only option for achieving what the company needed—but she'd been confident Renner would relent.

Now…was there any reason for her and Duke to remain married? His end of the agreement had been physical. A way to make them exclusive with no exceptions. But he'd saddled himself with a wife in the heat of the moment. If he had any regrets, here was the way out. Would he take it? She'd told him last night that he didn't need husband status to have the kind of no-strings relationship he wanted. Why wouldn't he sign? They were fellow commitment-phobes, weren't they? This was a windfall for them, right?

Familiar panic pressed at the front of her throat.

She threw an awkward gesture toward the open folder. "When did you have time…" Samantha began, shaking her head when she realized how lame those words sounded. She'd hinted on the phone that morning to Renner that she and Duke were together. He had lawyers on retainer that could have confirmed that information within minutes and prepared the paperwork.

"Look, you're not the first person to make a bad decision in Atlantic City. Have a little too much to drink and stumble into a chapel. Happens all the time." Renner nudged the folder in her direction. "It was a mistake to make marriage a condition of our contract. God knows any mention of the broken institution breaks me out in hives. You know I only ever want what's best for you."

"You sound like a dad," she muttered.

"Neither one of us knows what a dad is supposed to sound like." His expression stiffened, just for a brief moment, before reverting to its typical coolness. But the iciness was familiar. And that familiarity reminded her what a steady presence he'd been in her life. Distant but *constant.* Her *only* constant. But what he said next made her memories waver. "If you're going to be an effective member of this company's board, I'd rather have you single than married to an employee."

Samantha noticed Duke's flinch and realized she'd been intentionally naïve. She hadn't really expected Renner to be okay with her marrying one of his workmen, had she? No. She'd married Duke with blinders on, because deep down… she'd wanted to.

"It looks bad, Samantha. For me. For you." Her brother leaned forward, snaring her with the weight of his gaze. "Sign the paperwork."

"I'm not signing anything because you demand it. I'm just thinking. Give me a minute, all right?" She wanted to pick up Duke's hand, warm it with her breath, but she couldn't read him. He'd gone so still, staring at Renner like he'd strangle him with little encouragement. What did *that* mean? Perhaps he resented Renner's tactics, but he hadn't exactly spoken up and asked her *not* to sign. Why was she delaying? Any longer and it would seem as if…as if she wanted to remain married to Duke for another reason. Besides the money.

Since we're being truthful with each other, Sam, I'd rather swim in shark infested waters than date. Duke had spoken those very words the night they'd met. And she'd married him? God, she must be some kind of *lunatic.* How soon until he got sick of her and wanted to distance himself? A day? A month?

"*Samantha.*" Duke's voice reached through her thoughts, halting them the way a train screeches when the emergency break is applied. "You don't have to do a damn thing, sweetheart. You understand me? Let's go somewhere and talk. Just you and me."

Talking was what she wanted to avoid. Hearing the words "maybe it's for the best" grumbled from Duke's mouth. Because this man wanting to sever ties with her so soon? It sent her flying back to age fourteen, hiding in the closet of her stepdad's house while the U-Haul was loaded. But it was different, too.

Different because…she'd fallen for Duke. No sense in pretending he hadn't wrapped those big arms around her and ruined her for the entire world. It would be a unique brand of hurt, compared to what she'd experienced. Already a pit was opening and yawning wide in her stomach.

"Hudson is back in town already, Samantha, and he wants to see you." Renner spread his hands wide over the desk. "He doesn't have to know about any of this. No one does. But you should be free to make an alternate choice."

Hudson? Was he serious? She'd barely thought about the man, unless they were speaking on the phone. Her feelings had never developed past a mild crush and even that had been fleeting, despite his being a good man.

"Stop. Talking," Duke ground out, his blunt finger stabbing the air toward Renner. "I don't want to hear that fucker's name again. I don't want *her* to hear it."

"Why?" Renner's eyes sparked. "Because it's a reminder she can do better?"

"Yes," Duke murmured, so low she almost thought she'd imagined it. Was this about his ego or did he still want Samantha for himself? The trust she'd felt walking into the office gained a few more cracks.

Renner shook his head. "What are you thinking, holding her back like this? If you don't have aspirations of graduating to a management position, what exactly is your motivation?"

Duke's silence cut right through Samantha like a blade. After a moment, he turned a measuring look on her and she knew. She'd managed to accomplish everything she'd set out to avoid. He was going to drop her like a bad habit and there was no way to avoid the impact. She was tied to the train tracks and the engine was bearing down in her direction. Knowing too well what was coming, she beat it to the punch. "Sign it."

She picked up a pen, dropping it in her obvious haste, and banged her head on the desk's edge upon straightening. Duke made a sympathetic noise. "Come here, sweetheart," he rumbled, starting to reach for her, but she jerked back, shoving the pen into his hand.

"Just sign it. I…let's get this over with." She struggled to draw a breath. "I mean, mission accomplished and all that, so let's just end this before it ends itself."

Making the demand wasn't easy, so she was grateful when her brother spoke up again. But she didn't expect the compassion and defeat in his tone. It made everything worse. "Samantha." Renner's shoulders deflated in a very uncharacteristic way. "I, shit...I know what you're seeing here. In breaking the contract. But this is nothing like what happened with my father."

Jesus. The reminder of her most painful life experience twisted the blade Duke had already shoved between her ribs. "I know. I know that," she said too loudly. When had she jumped to her feet? She didn't know, but both Duke and Renner followed suit, both of them launching unwelcome concern in her direction. She was trapped. Nowhere to go. And she'd trapped Duke in return. "If you don't want to sign first, I will."

Duke refused to hand over the pen, holding it out of her reach, so she snatched up another one and signed where a red sticker had indicated she should. "There. Your t-turn."

"I didn't ask for a turn, Samantha," Duke said in a calming tone, advancing on her. Trying to fix the situation, as was his nature. Didn't he see it would only break again eventually? "Slow. Down."

Why wouldn't he just rip off the Band-Aid? The panic bubble that had been rising since—when? Last night? This morning?—burst, and she spoke without thinking. "We both know he's right. I wasn't thinking clearly last night or I would have seen that..." She clutched at her throat. "You can't support me. You'll only hurt this business. Through *me*. So just sign it and let's forget it ever happened."

When Duke jerked back like she'd slapped him, Samantha wanted to die. Just die right there on the floor. Or she thought she did, until Duke clicked the pen once and bent down to write his name beside hers on the contract. That. *That* was when she really wanted to lay down and never stand up.

An awful sob was her final word on the subject as she grabbed her belongings and jogged from the room, down the stairs, and through the silent factory, ignoring the security guard's concern when she passed him on the sidewalk outside. She forced herself to have tunnel vision as she took back streets toward the bus station...and whispered a prayer of relief when a bus arrived immediately after she'd purchased her ticket. It wasn't until she threw herself into the back row that she let herself cry.

• • •

Letting Samantha run from the room without going after her sent Duke straight back to the dry, dusty battlefield overseas. The need to *act* but unable to do so without a direct order or knowing what damage would be caused? Or had *already* been caused? That awareness was so fucking acute, he had to shove a hand up against his stomach so nothing would spill out.

Nothing Duke had in his wheelhouse would have broken through the state she'd been in. And he'd severely underestimated how deep her fears ran. She'd been almost breathtaking in her need to escape. Wild-eyed and ready to lash out. At him. Worse, she'd been right. Marrying Samantha had been a selfish act, pure and simple. No denying it. He'd wanted her for his own with such a powerful thirst...he'd taken her, damn the consequences.

Well, here they were. He was without a wife and his chest threatened to crumble, right along with the organ it housed. Not yet, though. Not until he knew the pieces at play. Obviously, he'd made the mistake of coming to this meeting unprepared, and knowing he'd gone into it uninformed only added insult to injury.

"What was that?" Duke rasped.

Renner sounded weary when he answered. "What was what?"

"*That.*" Duke roared the syllable. "I know she doesn't like having responsibility toward another person, but that wasn't Samantha. Saying…" Fuck. His chest ached. "Saying what she said to me. True or not. She didn't want to say it."

"No. She didn't." Renner scooped up the folder, scanning the signature lines, and laughing at what Duke had written, before tossing it back on the desk with a curse. "When Samantha and I became step-siblings, our parents were in love. Over the top in fucking love. You couldn't get away from it, even at the breakfast table, which is just…" He shivered. "My father legally adopted Samantha and they became close. He took her to the office, rained attention on her. Because it made Samantha's mother happy. Only, the happiness didn't last. Shocker, there. And during their ugly divorce, my father reversed Samantha's adoption. Because he's a bastard." Renner tapped his fist on the desk. "Samantha didn't handle it well. My father deserves most of the blame, but her mother didn't make it easy, using Samantha to guilt him, using her daughter's withdrawn state every chance she could."

Duke thought all the way back to the first night. Samantha's sadness over his sisters all being divorced. The glimpses of terror he'd seen in her just that morning, when he tried to delve deeper, get her to open up. And now… how she'd reacted to him clicking the fucking pen. *God.* His hands balled into fists, but instead of pummeling an object, he wanted to turn them on himself.

His first test and he'd failed with flying colors, hadn't he? He couldn't even blame the devil sitting behind the desk, because when he'd walked into the office, Samantha had been his semi-trusting wife. He'd vowed nothing in the world could reverse their progress or what they were on the verge of finding together. But she wasn't standing there anymore, was she?

The frustration collided with a fresh dose of anguish. The kind a man like Duke wasn't real fond of another man witnessing.

He turned on a heel, ready to go find Samantha, but Renner's words forced him to a stop in the doorway. "I really thought I was doing what's best for Samantha, you know." The fist he'd been tapping on the desk went flat. "I still think that."

"You're wrong," Duke managed past the doubt snaking around his jugular.

Renner's desk phone rang. "I don't envy you the task of proving me wrong." He paused a second before picking up the receiver. "Oh, and you're fired."

Duke's laughter didn't hold a single trace of humor. "Good luck with that."

Chapter Fifteen

Duke sat in the basement of his house, under the single glow of a light bulb where it hung from the ceiling. Being upstairs had grown unbearable, his sisters fluttering around him like a bunch of demented moths. The amount of food they'd cooked in the last few days could have fed Hook's population, plus the next two neighboring towns. No problem. For once in his life, Duke's appetite was non-existent. Nothing existed, really, except this king-sized pain bubble that had closed in on him from all sides, pushing his ribs and organs and muscles to the center, smashing them all until he could just sit there. Just sit there.

And stare down at the sketchpad he'd bought. It sat in front of him on the workbench, the blank white page illuminated by the bulb. He wondered what Samantha would say if she knew the impression she'd made that first night in The Third Shift with her drawing. When he'd walked into the stationary shop to purchase the pad, he'd gotten a sympathetic look from the woman behind the counter. Apparently word had traveled fast through Hook about Goliath being taken down with a well-placed stone, right between the eyes.

What would she say? If she were sitting there right now?

No, really, he needed to know. Because the silence was so fucking *silent* without her. Every second without her voice was like nails raking down his neck. He closed his eyes and huffed out a breath, picturing her on the stool beside him, adorable in her stop motion animation. Twirling her hair, realizing what she was doing, stopping, tapping her foot instead. Thinking, always thinking.

Who was the best babysitter in the Bible? she would ask.

I don't know, he would respond, settling her on his lap, taking a whiff of the smooth patch of skin behind her ear.

David, she would whisper. *He rocked Goliath to sleep.*

Duke grabbed the sketch pad with the intention of throwing it across the room and maybe pacing for a few hours. Again. No one could see him down there, which was how he wanted it. Also probably a good thing, considering he was wearing boxer shorts and socks. Nothing else.

The basement was good. It was dark and quiet. It matched the landscape inside of Duke. Desolate. Empty except for this sketchpad, the only object he'd been able to find that reminded him of Samantha. He kept staring, waiting for the answer to form on the page. Maybe…maybe he had to *make* it happen.

Duke plucked a thick work pencil from the old coffee can sitting on the table, pressing the tip down onto the page. Long minutes passed while he envisioned her face, how it had looked in the sunshine, while she wore his shirt. And he started to draw—

"All right. This shit has gone on too long."

"It's like a morgue in here. Should I be wearing a shroud? Who died?"

"Our brother."

"Oh, right. Right. We're in *mourning*."

Duke slammed his fist down on the table, snapping the pencil in half. "Get out."

Luanne stumbled back on the concrete ground, gasping with enough drama to power Broadway for a year. "Oh my God, he lives. He lives!"

A sniff over his shoulder. "I don't know. He smells pretty dead."

"What do you want?" Hell, he really did sound like a wounded animal, but he couldn't do anything about it. "Did your hairdryers blow a fuse again?"

They were silent so long, Duke frowned over, just in time for Lisa to swagger forward and drop a piece of paper in front of him with a flourish. "We coordinated. Our dryer schedules." She tapped the schedule with a long red fingernail, but Duke must have taken too long to comment, because Lisa threw a curse at her sisters. "You said this was going to work."

"What do I know about cheering a man up?" Lorraine mumbled. "My marriage was the shortest out of the four."

"Yeah, but my husband had the shortest—"

Duke smacked the table with his fist again, imploring the shadowed ceiling of his basement for patience. "Thank you for the schedule. Please go."

"Come on," Lacey said, dropping her chin onto his shoulder. "Talk to us. We're really worried. You haven't watched SportsCenter since—"

"Fuck SportsCenter." Shocked gasps filled the basement, but he ignored them, because now that he'd opened his mouth, everything rushed out, like a knife had slashed one of those big, bouncy castles they'd had in town over the summer. "I knew it, all right? I knew I couldn't be enough. Or be a better man than the rest of them. Your husbands, our father." He stood up, kicking the stool against the table. "I just *stood* there while she was drowning and I couldn't fix it. Didn't know *how*. And even if I could have said the right thing, what about next time? I'll never be able to keep it up. Being what she needs every single time. I didn't even ask her to marry me the right way. The way she deserved." His hands came up to drag down his face. "I've already let her down and we were only married one day. Oh *God*, you should have seen her—"

"You married Sam?"

"Did you even consider inviting us, or…"

"Shush," Luanne snapped. "We'll torture him for that when he's done being tortured by this." She tiptoed forward and laid a hand on Duke's shoulder. "What you just said was the biggest goddamn pile of nonsense I've ever heard."

"That was much better, Luanne."

Luanne held up a finger. "Look at you, Duke. Taking on the mistakes of other men as if you made them yourself. Stinking up the basement because you're heartsick over our Sam. Worried about how *she's* feeling, instead of yourself. There's your first clue you're one of a kind, brother. There's no one like you."

Lacey approached, laying her cheek in the center of his spine. "We have jobs, you know. We can afford our own place. But you gave us a home; you've always been the one to give us that."

"You did it for all of us," Lorraine said with a nod. "You can do that for Sam."

A teary-eyed Lisa blew out a shaky breath. "And she can do it for you, too."

Duke closed his eyes and pictured Samantha making a sandwich in his kitchen, or hell, *him* making one in *her* kitchen. He didn't care, as long as he could see and touch and *talk* to her. Could he continue to deserve that privilege, though? For the rest of his life, without hurting her? Without letting her down?

There was only one way to find out. And there might be stumbles along the way as they learned each other more.

Figured out this thing called marriage *their* way, without letting the negative feelings they'd been raised with get in the way. But they *would* learn. Because when a woman like Samantha agreed to be your wife, you didn't let her go. *God.* A woman like Samantha…

Duke glanced over his sisters' heads at the sketch pad. "I have an idea."

• • •

Samantha sat on a bench in Washington Square Park, peeling the crust off her tuna fish sandwich. Since returning from New Jersey a few days prior, she'd been living underwater. Everything seemed to be moving at a methodical pace — including herself — her co-workers voices reaching her from a distance, like they were calling to one another from inside a bleak, never ending tunnel. A void existed between her neck and thighs. She refused to let anything live there. Not easy. Not when a rake sat at the base of her neck, just waiting to scrape down and tear everything to ribbons.

It was stupid. Stupid to feel so empty over something that had happened in another time and place, so far away that words spoken and ideas borne in the dark felt like someone *else* had issued them. Had she left the city and married a virtual stranger? Yes. And he was still out there. Just not *here*. He was somewhere right now, smelling of musk and engine grease. That's the elusive combination of scents she'd settled on. She swore the smell emanated from every street corner. A poltergeist that had inhabited her personal space instead of a creepy movie house.

If a friend came home from a weekend away claiming she'd fallen for a man during the hiatus, Samantha would nod and smile but secretly wonder if that friend also believed in Bigfoot and Oompa Loompas. And yet, if she allowed the rake poised to shred her organs slip down, Samantha knew the gardening tool would encounter a big ball of woe and sadness where her heart used to beat, ripe to be torn away. She couldn't let her eyelids drift shut without remembering his chest hair on her back that single night they'd slept in the same bed. Or the way he'd instructed her not to chew the seats of his truck. What a man.

She couldn't even be mad at him. Which *sucked*. He'd been honest from the get-go. Maybe she was the one who had lied. Because for all her commitment issues, she'd been magnetized by Duke the moment they locked eyes. Even now, she battled the urge to ride the bus back to Hook, just to confirm the man with four sisters and a disposition that softened…only for her…was real. He must be. The entirety of her sketchbook was filled with him. It wouldn't hurt so much if he'd merely been another one of her imaginings.

Oh, God. The rake was slipping.

Samantha took a tasteless bite of her sandwich, just as her cell phone rang. At first, she resisted removing the device from her pocket. Renner was likely calling again. To apologize? To lecture her? She didn't feel like finding out, and as per usual, he neglected to leave a voicemail every time he phoned…

Wait. That wasn't her brother's ringtone, though. A generic one jangled, vibrating against her hip. *Duke Duke Duke.* An awful ripping feeling started at her neck, wreaking havoc down through her breast—just by allowing the hope to appear—but Samantha fought through, digging out her phone and answering the unknown number, the park falling into slow motion around her.

"H-Hello?"

"Samantha?" A woman's voice. One that sounded familiar, but her mind took a moment to recognize through the sharp disappointment. "It's River."

"River," she rasped, tossing her sandwich at an aggressive-looking squirrel. "You're real."

Warm laughter smoked through the connection. "You don't sound well. Are you sick?"

"No, I'm fine." Samantha pressed two fingers against her lips to keep a sob contained. *Don't ask about him. Don't do it.* "I'm just feeding the squirrels."

"Oh. Okay." A heavy pause where Samantha could feel humiliation blooming in her midsection, but not enough to backpedal or attempt to make sense. Too much effort. "You left Hook pretty quickly. We didn't have a chance to say good-bye."

"I know. I'm sorry." Samantha slumped down on the bench, resting her head along the painted green iron, wondering how she could feel twice as lonely now that she was actually speaking to another human being. "How is Marcy?"

"Great." There was so much affection in the single word, Samantha had to close her eyes. "She's the reason I'm calling, actually."

Her eyelids lifted as premonition trickled into her gut. "Oh. Why?"

"Well…" She could practically hear River gulp. "I know a bunch of three- and four-year-olds isn't your typical age group, but…the way you drew her dream house? I showed it to Marcy's teacher and she would love to have you come in, to do the same for the rest of her class?"

Samantha turned onto her side, lying lengthwise on the bench. Probably catching some rare disease but unable to feel concerned. "Come back to Hook?"

There was a patient smile in River's voice when she responded. "Yes, it would require some traveling. It's just…it would mean so much. To the kids."

Could she return to Hook so soon? What if she ran into Duke?

Yowza. Even thinking his name, picturing him standing

on the curb as she alighted from the bus, made every blood vessel in her body twirl and sing like a manic Disney character. Would he still want to get naked and sweaty with her? Yeah. Yeah, she didn't think that would change any time soon. For either of them. But she'd totally shown her hand in the meeting. A person didn't lose their crap the way she'd done, unless other feelings were in play. And she'd recruited a whole team of them. First *and* second sting.

So, should she turn River down? Miss the opportunity to do what she loved for a bunch of sweet nursery school kids… and label herself a coward in the process? No. She wouldn't do that. Because Duke wouldn't be there. The town wasn't so small that she couldn't avoid running into him for a couple hours, right?

Why did she kind of hope that assumption proved incorrect?

"Uh…" Samantha sat up, pushing the hair out of her eyes. "When were you thinking?"

Chapter Sixteen

It was Monday morning and Samantha had arranged with her boss to work off-site for the day. Not terribly unusual for an illustrator, but rather odd for Samantha, who tended to never miss a day. Turned out that reliability worked in her favor, because her boss hadn't so much as batted an eyelash at her request. There had been a brief flash of hope that he would protest, thus giving Samantha an excuse to back out of traveling to Hook. But no. Here she was with a satchel and two tote bags full of art supplies, one stop from the New Jersey town she'd fled from over a week ago. After signing annulment papers from a man with whom she had a bunch of unresolved and unrelenting feelings. Yeah. Totally normal.

Deep breath.

Ever since River's call, she'd no longer been able to pretend the weekend in Hook had been a crazy, beautiful dream. As a result, she'd become restless, forgetting where she put things, feeling as if she were late for something. *All the time.* Even though she knew it wasn't true.

When the bus screeched to a halt, so did Samantha's

stomach. The bus driver gave her a lazy nod, which she returned while shouldering her supplies and walking to the exit, knees knocking loud enough for someone to answer. River had texted directions from the terminal to Marcy's nursery school, so she knew it was only a brief, ten-minute walk, but trudging through the close-knit town while cars and people passed? Made her feel like a gunslinger returning to the OK Corral after killing the sheriff or something.

A visual of herself with a low-slung six-shooter, maybe a patch over her right eye, brought the beginnings of a smile to Samantha's lips, but it quickly vanished when the nursery school came into view. She tripped into a halt on the sidewalk, her mind attempting to process everything in sight.

The squat, brick building was decorated with balloons — bright pinks, greens, and yellows. Picnic tables had been set up in the grassy courtyard, but there were so many children — of all ages — they continued out into the street, giving the appearance of a block party. As if cued up by her arrival, music began to drift down the street, festive and inviting. There were female voices, too. Ones she'd replayed frequently over the last week, attempting to mimic, just for the sake of keeping their owners fresh and real. Duke's sisters. They corralled children, throwing paper plates in front of them, pouring giant Costco-sized cartons of Goldfish crackers into bowls.

At the street's center, a long strip of white — possibly poster board or even…sheetrock? — had been set up for a group of older kids. Holding paintbrushes, each of them worked on a different section of the colorful mural, which was already beautiful in its total randomness.

But it was the sign in the front yard of the school that made her heart whip into a blur of beats. It had been connected on each end to a tree, the white paper drifting up and down in the summer breeze. SAM'S ART DAY. Somehow she knew Duke had painted on the words, because they were in all caps and no-nonsense. And her suspicion of his involvement was further confirmed when he ducked under the sign, carrying a stacked handful of paint pallets.

Samantha wanted to run back toward the bus. The exact *opposite* of the reaction she should have been having to something so incredible. The tote bags slipped off her shoulders, making her body feel light—aerodynamic—encouraging the instinct. What was happening? Had Duke planned it? If so…what did that mean?

As if her distressed thoughts were appearing above her head like firecrackers, Duke's head turned, gaze pinning Samantha. And time ground to a halt.

The rake that had been sitting at the base of her neck plowed downward, shredding everything in its wake. She couldn't even claim temporary insanity over the hasty marriage, because seeing him again stuck her right back in the middle of the swirling eddy of that weekend. And this impulse to keep Duke at a distance wasn't even about him signing papers to end their marriage. No, it was the fact that he had the power to hurt her at all. Having him close only confirmed that power he held.

Was this art day…this breathtaking creation from her dreams…his way of apologizing? To what end?

"Samantha," Duke's voice boomed.

Her spine snapped straight at his warning tone. "Yes?"

Ohhh and then he crooked his finger at her. *Get over here.*

"Presumptuous," she called, her voice thinner than usual, because God—and her body—knew she *loved* when he went all commanding. If the clenching of her thighs was any indication, the former wouldn't be forgetting any time soon. There was no way Duke would let her turn tail and get on the bus this time. His battle-ready stance indicated that in spades.

When Marcy ran up and tugged on Duke's white T-shirt, he picked her up with one arm, without even looking. His lips moved and whatever he said to the little girl had her tiny hand waving at Samantha across the street.

"Come over here, Samantha!" Marcy called.

Oh boy. So they were playing dirty, were they?

Terrified at what lay ahead, Samantha wrapped the last remaining strand of courage around her fist and walked across the street.

Toward her ex-husband and current, kind of, maybe obsession. Not to mention the man she could, under no circumstances, allow back in to hurt her a second time. This was going to sting.

• • •

Duke watched River greet Samantha at the front gate to the nursery school, setting down Marcy so she could run over and join the introductions that had hit the ground running. *Jesus Lord.* He was in trouble. Samantha was a gorgeous woman under any circumstances, but *his* case was specialized. Not having laid eyes on her sun-licked skin and sweet smile in over a week, then having her presented in front of him, like a live, moving snapshot from his every dream, had Duke tied into an unbreakable knot within seconds.

God, I missed you, sweetheart.

Didn't seem possible how much. She hadn't even been a part of his life two weeks ago. Thank God the planning for Sam's Art Day had given him something positive to focus on. Otherwise, he might still be living in his basement, wearing boxer shorts, and eating his fifth box of Nilla Wafers, trying to figure out how the fuck everything had gotten away from him.

And it wasn't *just* about getting her back now. Although, truth be told, if the day ended without Samantha in his house, in his sheets, in his life, he wouldn't know what the fuck to do with himself. But the art day was about making Samantha happy, too. Knocking the memory of her forlorn expression out of his head for good, because blinking without seeing it had turned impossible.

I'm a goddamn mess, Duke wanted to shout at her.

Right. Because that would bring her running back.

Samantha drifted into the courtyard a touch farther, crouching down to shake the kids' hands. Murmuring hellos to his sisters, who weren't satisfied until they'd damn near lifted her off the ground in a bear hug. And every few seconds, her gaze drifted over to him, gliding over his face, his shoulders, like the touch of her skillful hand, which he remembered so well.

Yes, sir. He was in trouble. Because if she got within two feet of him, he'd embarrass himself. The way a fan waiting for an autograph might. This was the woman who'd agreed to marry him, by some crazy stroke of luck, and he'd failed to even keep her for a single damn day. So he needed to focus all of his energy on being worthy in her eyes again, instead of devising methods to get her alone, preferably somewhere hundreds of kiddy eyes weren't watching.

Once he tried his hand at making her happy, he'd see what he could do about the rest. As in, taking the broken trust between them and patching it back together.

Finished greeting Duke's sisters and meeting the school volunteers, Samantha took a few steps closer, forehead wrinkling when she saw him in her path, before turning in a circle, chewing her thumbnail. While she set down her bags—damn, why hadn't he helped her with those?—Duke positioned himself behind the closest table, hoping it would serve as a reminder not to scoop up Samantha and carry her home.

"Hey, Sam."

Her answering smile was more like a flinch. "Hi, Duke."

"You look pretty," Duke said, halfway through a swallow,

wishing he'd watched a little less SportsCenter over the last
decade and a lot more Lifetime. "You're always pretty."

"Th-Thank you." Samantha stared at Duke like he'd
turned green. Maybe he had. But when she transferred her
attention to the swingy, strapless, blue dress she wore—as if
she didn't know it did fucking *everything* for her body—Duke
wanted to shake her. He'd never seen anyone or anything
more stunning in his life and he never would. Just another
reason there was a table located between them.

"Uh, yeah." He scratched at the hair over his ear. "Stations.
You told me you wanted stations, so I broke it up. You'll be
over there, drawing their stories, the way…the way you do,
sweetheart." He threw his hand out to indicate the shaded
tree, under which he'd set out a blanket and some chairs, in
case some of the other kids wanted to see her in action—and
who wouldn't? "Lacey is doing something involving Popsicle
sticks over at one table. I'm going to paint faces—"

"You're going to what?"

"Paint faces, Sam." He winked at her. "Try and keep up."

"I missed…" She half laughed half whispered, and Duke
swore he'd been harpooned square in the chest. "I missed
the way you talk to me. No one does that." While he held his
breath, she looked out at the moving colors and rambunctious
neighborhood kids. "You had River dupe me. Why? Why did
you do all this?"

"You *know* why." Duke wanted to break the table in half
with his fist, just to reach her. "I'm sorry for what happened.
Sorry about how it went down. Sorry about the result, because
it sent you packing. *Away* from me."

"I was *always* going to leave Hook. That was the deal,
right?" One of the adult volunteers passed by with bakery
boxes and Samantha ducked her head, rooting through one
of her tote bags—which had the words "Turnip the Beat" in
script over a dancing purple vegetable. "We were only going

to see each other occasionally—"

"The lies we tell ourselves, right?" Duke planted a hand on the table and leaned across. "You were never going to spend a single night out of my bed, once I got you there. We both said those vows knowing it, too."

Her eyes went bright and a little languid, the way he remembered them on the hotel room balcony, when his erection had been tucked up beneath her ass. "Vows," she repeated, her tone duller than the word deserved. "Duke, what you put together here is really special. It's so beautiful. Thank you."

His jaw ached from being clamped so tight. "I hear the *but* in there and I'm not accepting it."

The tension pumping out of their conversation must have been obvious, because River stepped into the space beside Samantha, sliding an arm across her shoulders. "Hey, let's go grab a cup of coffee and get to our stations. The elementary school kids only have an hour before they have to leave."

"Oh," Samantha said with a nod. "We should get started, then."

With a final look up at Duke through the filter of her eyelashes, she turned and found her spot beneath the tree. It took him a while to relax enough to take his own station. The reminder that the day was young was the only thing that got him through an afternoon of watching Samantha's hair sail in the breeze, her hand moving across the page…smiles directed everywhere but at him.

Fear beat in his throat. She was closed off. Not going to listen.

The realization that he'd have to *make* Samantha listen heated his blood, even as he wondered at the wisdom of his next course of action. When he looked at the woman he'd married in that closet-sized Atlantic City chapel—a place so unworthy of her—he saw her through a memory of a much older man. The man he would be in thirty years, remembering back to the week they'd met. His fate wasn't getting away from him. Maybe right now, when they were so new, their insane physical connection was all he had to break through the wall she'd built. Be he wouldn't let that be *all* he used. He had the right words stored up, ready to spill. He just needed her to listen. He'd do everything in his power to make it happen.

As if Samantha could hear his intentions click into place, her eyes lifted to him and widened.

Chapter Seventeen

Nothing had ever been important enough to divert Samantha's attention from a child's story. Even now, she was picked up and tossed about in their imaginations, one by one. She loved every cute, stinking minute. But damn it all if how Duke's brow wrinkled in concentration as he painted a stick figure unicorn on Marcy's face didn't have her awareness torn in two very different halves.

They were on opposite ends of the courtyard, but she might as well have been sitting on his lap for the effect that seeing him again had on her. She'd spent a week wondering if he'd been real at all, now there he sat, bigger and better than her memories. And if she'd had any doubts that Duke still wanted her, they were laughable now. He made sure she was aware of him with every downward sweep of his hot, observant gaze, increasing the tickle in her stomach until it spread over her skin, sensitizing and raising gooseflesh. Not good.

Not good, because it wasn't only about sex between them. He'd made that clear when she arrived. Maybe she'd been fooling herself or denying the burn she, too, felt deep down in her chest, but it was *so* there. Attempting to grow brighter, except she'd thrown a shroud over it, hoping to subdue the light, because he'd proven in the meeting how easily he could scale her defenses.

Never again.

Samantha tore her attention off Duke and thought she heard him make a frustrated sound. Time was moving too quickly. The line of students had dwindled down to one and his drawing of a basketball court in his neighborhood—complete with two-story high Gatorade coolers—was nearly completed. No way Duke was letting her get back on the bus without another confrontation, and with the volunteers clearing away the decorations and folding up chairs already, they were going to be alone before she was ready. Before she'd gotten up the determination to resist whatever he threw her way.

Twenty minutes later, the elementary school children were lined up at the front gate, showing off their sketches to one another, while the instructors took a harried headcount. River had vanished into the nursery school, aiding the teachers with getting the younger kids settled once again, despite their excitement at having painted faces and Popsicle-stick animals in their hands. For her part, Samantha might as well have been fleeing a crumbling building, shoving supplies into her bags while Duke's eyes burned a hole in her back. God, she could even feel them licking up her thighs, wishing for access beneath her dress. This was insane. She couldn't let him sink her back down into the quicksand like last time, when she'd lost entire days to some bogus hunch that Duke was somehow different than every other human being on the planet.

Duke's hand slid over Samantha's hip, just as the summer breeze kicked up, absorbing her moan. She froze in the act of stuffing her pencil case into the tote bag, swaying forward like someone completely out of control of their own body. And maybe she was. Because instead of turning around and making her desire to leave clear, Samantha held her breath and waited, waited to hear what he'd say next.

"Leave your things here." Duke's stubble scraped against Samantha's ear and she almost had a full-on orgasm just at the reminder of his coarse body. "Walk with me."

"Where are we going?" She swallowed hard. "I mean… where would we go, if I agreed to walk with you?"

"Just the church around the corner." His palm twisted on her hipbone, then squeezed tight. "Nothing too bad can happen in church, can it?"

Samantha was skeptical, but her body desperately wanted to accept the justification for spending time with Duke, no matter what they ended up doing. Talking, staring one another into a stupor…other *things*. Truthfully, she just *missed* him with her whole self, starting with the organ pumping inside her ribcage, those vibrations resonating lower and lower, until her thighs clenched so tight she worried walking might not even be an option. *Can you carry me? I'm too sexually aroused by your stubble to walk.* That would be cute.

No. *No.* She needed to be stronger than her libido. Come hell or high water, she was going back to Manhattan today. Either she accomplished that with a renewed sense of pride in her own restraint, or with a little piece of her heart chipped away. That's what would happen, right? If she gave over her entire self again then had to go on without him?

"I can't," she said hoarsely, sucking in a breath when his teeth closed around her earlobe. "I need to go, Duke."

"Fine. Get on the bus. I'm coming with you, though," he gritted out. "I'll crowd you right up against the window the whole damn way until we talk everything out."

The flip-flop in her chest was practically audible. "Why

can't we talk it out right here?"

Pain laced his low laughter. "Because I'm in the middle of a fucking Samantha drought…and I've finally got the entire reservoir of you right in front of me." He breathed a sigh into the crook of her neck. "I don't want to share a single drop with anyone else. And I don't want to give you an avenue of escape, either. I already did that once and I'm not giving you the option of leaving me miserable from missing you again. Not until you hear me out."

"Okay," she whispered, her knees weak. "Okay, let's walk."

· · ·

Duke performed maintenance at the church on a regular basis. Adeline, the choir director, had been a Hook fixture since Duke was a young kid, and you flat-out didn't tell the woman no. Not unless you wanted a guilt trip heaped on your head every time she passed you in town. *Oh, I'm fine…apart from the chill in my bones, since no one has been by to repair the heat.* Uh-uh. Not to mention, Duke had a soft spot for the lady, since she'd stopped by with dinners after their father left, all those years ago, when his mother had been sapped of energy.

Being the designated handyman meant Duke had keys to the church's back office and knowledge that no one would be inside the establishment until later that evening, for the weekly youth group. Good knowledge to have, considering Samantha walked alongside him, the hem of her dress floating up in the breeze, just like the pretty ends of her hair. She'd attempted to pull away when Duke had taken her hand and remained stiff now, even though she continued to throw glances in his direction from the corner of her eye. Longing ones that told Duke exactly what would happen when they got inside the church office. Yeah, his cock was already hardening in preparation—for disappointment—because her heart, not her body, was where his focus needed to be.

The brick wall around her, mortared by fear, was tangible. It cut his need with a desperation to make everything right. And he would. But it required more than a simple explanation. Even if the meeting with Renner had gone perfectly, she would still have been skeptical of his intentions. Mainly because he hadn't been honest, with Samantha or himself. So he needed to do more than just explain. He needed to *convince*. After today, he hoped she would never have to question him again.

They reached the gray clapboard church, but instead of walking through the front double doors, Duke led Samantha around back, his pulse beginning to spike and dip, knowing they'd be alone soon. Behind closed doors. When he stopped at the back entrance and pulled out his set of keys, Samantha tugged free of his opposite hand, folding her arms with a smirk.

"Well *this* feels orchestrated."

Duke slid in the key, pushed open the door, and guided Samantha inside, drawing a greedy breath of her scent. "It is."

He watched the ticking at the base of her neck accelerate when a dark, empty hallway greeted them. "Don't bother denying it or anything," she whispered.

"I meant what I said. I didn't want you running off on me again." He cupped the back of her neck as they walked, circling his thumb along her nape. "And I couldn't kiss you in front of a bunch of kids, either. So I had to think of something."

"Kissing." She threw him a heavy-lidded look over her shoulder as Duke urged her into the first room and closed the door, advancing on her. "Is that what you had in mind?"

Starved out of his goddamn mind for contact with her, Duke's ability to be gentle vanished as his body pinned Samantha to the far wall, just beside the ancient, oversized printer. "Yeah, it is. I've been dreaming about your mouth for a week." They both groaned as muscle and feminine curves fused together, Duke's erect cock wedging up against Samantha's belly. Already, it wasn't going as planned, with his body and heart teaming up to override his mind, but his hunger for this woman knew no reason. His hands grasped the sides of her face. "Give me what I've been missing."

Samantha's head fell back and Duke went in, giving no relief or room for backing out, his lips prying apart her softer ones. His tongue sliding past her defenses and taking, taking her drugging perfection. *I've been needing you so bad.* Their moans cracked right in the middle, unable to be sustained, when there was so much else. So much to taste. He felt Samantha's fingers curl in the bottom of his shirt, before traveling underneath to race up his chest, nails raking, palms smoothing. Fuck, *fuck*, he was going to lose his load right there in his underwear, just from their tongues twining together.

He jerked Samantha close but had to smack her ass back up against the wall at the devastating loss of friction, knees bending, hips pushing forward to grind his cock where it belonged. "Sam," he groaned into her mouth, trying to rein in his libido and failing. "*Sam.*"

She shoved at his shoulders, breaking away, alarm clear in her eyes, probably at the out and out agony in his voice. Lips puffy, cheeks red, expression dazed—but wary, dammit—she yanked his T-shirt up, suctioning her mouth to his right nipple, then the left. A bolt of hunger wrapped around his cock like a manacle as the slide of her lips moved lower, over his stomach and down his happy trail, accompanied by the drag of her fingertips. When her knees landed on the ground, she burrowed her cheek there, rubbing her face and whimpering into his abdomen.

Duke's head fell back on his shoulders, a battle waging between longing so fierce he couldn't believe it was real...

and his utter determination to do the right thing. To reach Samantha, bring her back to where he'd been stranded for a week. On an island without any means of survival. Without *her*. "Up, sweetheart. Please. Get up."

"You said you've been dreaming about my mouth." The sound of his zipper coming down forced Duke to brace himself with hands planted on the wall. Hands that turned to shaking fists when Samantha took out his dick, feathering the tip with a brush of her lips. *Christ.* "Did you mean this?"

"We've got plenty of time for sucking," Duke rasped. "But there's not enough hours in the day for how badly I need to hold you."

As if she hadn't heard him — or chose not to acknowledge — Samantha closed her mouth around his throbbing head, sucking like a lollipop, before gliding down, halfway to his base. She paused there, her shoulder bracing against his thighs, then she took the rest, not stopping until he encountered the back of her throat, the little whimper she released making his balls swell like a motherfucker.

A vile curse shook past his lips, the instinct to thrust so violent he had to tighten his fists until pain raced up his forearms. But the nights of loneliness, the bleak reality of not having Samantha, dropped down on his head, blanketing him in a denial. No, he wouldn't live like that. Wouldn't live without the woman who'd waltzed into his life and made a home in his chest. Wouldn't let her live without him, either.

With a burst of willpower, Duke's hands left the wall to hook beneath Samantha's arms, hauling her to her feet, using a flattened palm to press her back against the wall. Noting her shock, her multiplying panic. "I won't lie, sweetheart. I missed your mouth for all the dirty reasons. God knows I did." His hand slid up to cradle her cheek. "But that's not what kept me up at night. Kept me pacing, wondering who was going to make you coffee and scramble your eggs. Wondering if you take a safe route to work or if you're thinking of me, too. Yeah. I missed your mouth, because it guards your voice. And I fucking love your voice, Samantha."

Her fingers wrapped around his wrist, slowly, just holding on, but not trying to remove his touch.

"'Did you just set yourself up as a roadblock?' That's the first thing you said to me. And the way you sounded…it made me happy and sad and everything in between. Because it was like I'd just been waiting to hear you talk. And everything was beginning and ending right there. Like a crossroads." Damn, his throat already hurt from so much talking. Or maybe the crowded sensation came from the words themselves. "I am, you know. I'm *your* roadblock. And you're not getting through me."

Her head was shaking before Duke finished making his promise. "I already got through you. This w-was over before it started."

If she'd sounded even remotely convinced by her own breathless statement, Duke might have shouted or beat the wall with his fists, but the barriers she'd thrown up already had cracks. He'd delivered an effective blow and knew she needed time to reel, to regroup, so he would help her through, make her aware of his sincerity, if more than promises were required. His plan had been to talk—*just* talk—but if he could use their attraction just enough to get her attention and keep it, he would use what he had. He would use *anything*.

"Did you think you could come to town without seeing me?" His palms rasped along the hem of her dress, slowly beginning to gather the material, bunching it up around her hips. "Did you think I would let that happen?"

Her eyelids slipped closed. "I didn't know. I'm not sure of anything."

Patience. Duke took her mouth in a painfully slow kiss, the corresponding twist and shudder in his gut almost unbearable. He curved greedy hands over the swell of her ass cheeks, growling when she went up on her toes, tilting her hips and pushing the tight globes into his touch with a whimper. With an effort, he pulled away. "You're not sure of anything," he groaned. "You want to rephrase that?"

"I'm sure we'll make each other feel good," she breathed, doe eyes flashing.

"You're sure of a hell of a lot more than that." Duke tugged her thong down beneath her bottom, giving her a little double-tap to signal she get rid of them, which she did with a sexy little shimmy before kicking them away. "Getting you off is a foregone conclusion and I love you knowing that. Because it's true. It's my privilege." His fingers trailed down the smooth skin of her belly, circling her navel, drifting lower. "But there's more you need to be sure about. You need to know I'll take extra care cooking your steak on the grill every Sunday. That at the next barbeque I'll make sure you wear sunscreen, because your pretty skin got too red last time. You need to know I'll help shower it off you afterward, using my hands as a washcloth." His touch found her pussy and she gasped, her knee swinging up to prop against his hip. "Those are things you need to be sure about, sweetheart. My mouth finding yours for a kiss, no matter the audience. Chasing away men who think they're worthy of your puns. Egg sandwich runs late at night. Be sure of those things."

There was a tug-o-war playing out across Samantha's features, obviously spurred by so many potential certainties. And maybe she wanted to pretend the future wasn't being knitted with those words, wanted to simply let the lust take over and worry about the consequences later, but she was trying to struggle against the urge. It was there in the set of her chin, the fight in her eyes. He admired her all the more for that defensiveness, but nothing would stop him from toppling it, either.

Although, when she reached into his pocket, took out the condom, and ripped it open with her teeth, rolling it with painstaking slowness down his heavy dick, Duke's focus blurred like he'd been clocked by a right hook. "Think about right *now*. *Just* now." Finished covering him in latex, Samantha transferred her hands to her dress, folding the snug blue top down to reveal her tits, grazing the pink, pouting nipples with her fingertips. "Please, Duke?"

God help him, he would *not* lose his chance to keep Samantha from today forward. Sex would be a temporary fix, and using their attraction to convince her they should be together would do just that. So he would give her what she was angling for, up to a point, and then he'd make her listen. He was running out of options.

Resolve plowed into him, running alongside almost fanatical need, surging his body forward. He slung an arm beneath Samantha's hips and lifted, gratified when she released a cut-off scream, excitement and nerves ricocheting between them like pinballs. Those daydream legs of hers banded around his waist, her head falling back, teeth sinking into her upper lip, just waiting, *waiting* for that first thrust.

Duke didn't disappoint her. His cock sank home with a satisfying, wet, sliding sound, strangled moans clashing between them. "Yes," Samantha cried, clinging to his shoulders, clawing his neck, heels pushing down on his ass. "Yes, *please*. Duke, I'm—"

He silenced her pleas by ramming her sweet body up against the wall, gritting a curse when he sunk the final few inches to the hilt. *Mine. Still mine. Always mine.* "Look at me. Look me in the eye."

Samantha tensed, just a touch, dropping her chin and laying all that obvious need on Duke, filling him with purpose. More so, when he slid their damp lips together, breathing into her mouth, and she only melted, melted against him. Matching his drags of air as if she couldn't help it.

"Samantha," he said, packing steel into his voice. "Somewhere along the way, I stopped being afraid of commitment and started being afraid of losing you." Holding her astonished stare, he shook his head. "And that's not going to change. It's not going to change, no matter what pieces of paper are thrown into the mix. There is just us. And *I'm* committed to *you*. End of story."

"Duke—"

He started to fuck her, long, hot grinds of his cock deep inside the snug fit of her body. The sweetest fit ever created. He watched through the haze of lust as Samantha attempted to hold on to what she needed to say, eventually trading the urge in favor of moaning. His name. *Only* his name, for the rest of her life. He'd make sure of it. The certainty of that was such an incredible high that his filter shattered on the floor. "I'm going to *walk* you places, Samantha," he ground out into her hair, delivering tight pushes of his length, memorizing every whimper she let loose. "Church, work, restaurants, up the pathway to the house. I'm going to hold an umbrella over your head when it's raining. I'm going to carry you when you're sick. Carry your sketchbooks, too. I'll do that for my sweetheart. I'll do everything."

Duke only caught a split second of teary-eyed, blissed-out Samantha, before she yanked his head down for a kiss. A kiss that made his legs feel void of power, dipping their undulating bodies down, before he regained strength and shot Samantha back up against the wall. He tried to maintain the slow rhythm of his pumps, but having his woman's tongue in his mouth made him hungry, turning his hips to pistons, machines made for her pleasure. When she responded by arching her back and tweaking her hips in a tight circle, in a way Duke knew would rub her clit against his base, the pressure in his balls grew so intense, his jaw went slack.

"Oh my God," she wailed, her tits lifting and falling in hot, little bounces. "Right there, right there, *right there*."

Duke growled into the space above her head, forcing himself to hold his position and tempo until she came, even though his instincts demanded he pound her even faster, even harder into the wall, blur out the week he'd spent alone and frustrated. "I got you, Sam," he rasped. "I've always got you. Any second now those thighs are going to shake for me. You're going to buck your hips when it hits, trying to bring me along with you." He heard her breath begin to shallow, seizing and blowing out in warm gusts, knew she was close as hell. "You know why you think of getting me off, too, when you should be enjoying the ride? Because you *care*. You can't turn it off. Your heart is beautiful and it needs to give." He pressed a damp kiss beneath her ear, licked up the side of her neck. "I see you, sweetheart. Now see the only man who's going to give you everything in return."

A sob fell past her mouth, her knees jerking at his waist, incoherent words falling from her lips. "Duke. I-I…oh my *God*."

Pressing their foreheads together, he angled his hips to drive impossibly deeper, groaning at the way she started to contract around him, her thighs smooth and tight around his waist. *Christ*, she was perfection. "I was your warrior our first night, wasn't I, Sam?"

"Yes."

"That's what I'm going to be for the rest of my life. For you. Until you're sure of me, I'll go to battle and win my woman." He clamped his teeth down on her shoulder and lifted her high with his body, bouncing her on his dick. One, two, three… "Right now, my woman needs to come, doesn't she? Soak my dick with it, sweetheart. Give me the spoils of my fucking war."

"Yes. *Yes.*"

She went off like a bomb blast, screaming his name, trembling with such intensity, he almost felt sympathy for the pained pleasure she was going through.

But the reminder of pain, coupled with the relief of giving Samantha enough pleasure to make her pussy constrict like a fist, brought Duke's focus screaming back to his own oncoming sexual destruction. And that's exactly what it felt like when the thunderheads broke at the base of his spine, throwing him directly into the eye of the storm. "So good, so *good*. Oh...*fuck*."

Duke bit off the curse, hands working out of desperation to jerk Samantha's legs wide, giving Duke room to give his final brutal drives, pitching him over the cliff and hurtling back down the other side. He couldn't see through his eyes or hear any damn thing, apart from the ringing in his ears, for an interminable amount of beats. But Samantha's gasping breaths brought him back. Gradually at first. And then the sense of completion clawed inside his chest, right up into his throat.

He and Samantha. Clinging to one another. Exactly as it should be.

So much to say. *Has to be now.*

Unfortunately, that was when his cell phone started to vibrate in the pocket of his jeans, where they'd slumped down against his thigh.

Chapter Eighteen

Samantha was the definition of *plastered* up against Duke, because she could feel every single rattle of his phone. One of them needed to move, if not because the call must be urgent, then definitely because they couldn't stay locked together forever, attempting to come down from *uncomedownable* sex.

She flat out *was not* going to recover. Physically? Maybe sometime during the next full moon. But mentally…oh Lord, Duke had put her through the ringer. Because that dangerous flare of hope was back. The one she'd encountered in Atlantic City. Maybe even before. She'd managed to keep that optimism subdued, but even with both eyes open, he'd managed to stab her in the heart. Now—after he'd dangled those sweet promises in front of her eyes—how would she walk away again?

I'll carry you when you're sick…

With a choked sound, Samantha let her legs slip down Duke's sides, trying to extricate his hold. He wouldn't let her go, wouldn't let her take a single step. His arms caged her against the wall, that sensual mouth she'd watched fall open on a groan just moments earlier now set in a grim line.

"Now we talk."

Panic surged. "Shouldn't you answer the phone?"

His jaw ticked. "Everyone I want to talk to is right here."

Samantha could only stare as Duke picked up her hand, kissing the palm with warm lips.

"Samantha, listen to me. There's no denying this thing between you and me is crazy. I married you the night after we met." His breathing was careful, controlled. "But whether you want to believe it or not, we both knew it wasn't about some fucking arrangement. Okay? We knew. And you won't make me think differently if I live to be two hundred years old." Another, harder, branding of her palm before he laid her hand on the side of his face. "So I'm asking you to trust the crazy. I'm asking you to come live in my house, wear my ring, and be my wife. I'm asking you to *try*. If you're going to be scared, be scared with me. Where I can see you and touch you and tell you—*goddammit*—that I'm all in, sweetheart."

The sound of Duke's phone going off for the umpteenth time startled Samantha out of the stupor she'd been placed in by his speech. With a sound of extreme irritation, he reached between them to zip his pants and snatch the cell phone out of his pocket. While he checked the screen, eyebrows lifting, Samantha could only stare. She couldn't do as he asked, couldn't take that risk, could she? No...no it would never last. Both of their families were proof of that.

"Who..." She cleared the rust from her voice. "Who's calling?"

"Your brother."

"Why?"

Duke's laughter held a note of sarcasm. "That's a good question, considering he fired me last week."

Samantha jerked backward, bumping into the wall. "*What?*" She gathered her thoughts, but they came too slowly, like sticky wool. "Because of...of course. Of course it was because of me. I-I'm sorry. I should have known. I'll make it right—"

He laid a finger over her mouth with a *shhh* sound. "Hey, I can find another job. But I can't find another Samantha. All right?"

Her heartbeat tried to deafen her. "When did you start saying things like that?"

"You." He dropped his finger, searing her to the very core with the meaning in his gaze. "A lot of things started with you. I'm trying to make them end with you, too."

"*Duke.*" His name emerged like a plea. "I don't think I can do it. There was a safety release when we had our agreement. It meant short term. No strings to cut. But trying, *actually* trying...I don't think I can. I'm terrified."

"I know." He tucked the cell phone under his armpit, in favor of cradling Samantha's face in his hands. "I know. And that's why I didn't just clear up what really happened in that meeting as easily as I could have. Because knowing that annulment was never valid wouldn't have made you any less scared. Only we can do that. Together. Okay?"

Confusion moved in like fog, wrinkling Samantha's brow. "What—" Again, the phone went haywire and Duke's head fell forward. "Answer it," she forced out through lips that had lost their feeling. What really happened in the meeting? What did he mean?

"Crawford," Duke rumbled into the phone, still watching Samantha from lowered brows. "This better be good."

The sound of Renner's low, urgent reply—although the actual words weren't discernable—snagged Samantha's attention. Her brother never sounded concerned, only curious, calculating, or amused. Alarm stole up her middle in increments when Duke's body tensed, his big shoulders rolling back as he straightened. "Which machine is it...eight, huh? Shit." He listened a moment. "Damn right I know how to fix it, unless it's too late. How long has it been smoking?" Another pause, followed by a hollow laugh from Duke. "Yeah. That's the definition of too late."

Samantha laid a hand on Duke's arm on impulse, able to feel his nerves crowding across the scant separation between them. He looked down at where she touched him and moved closer, kissing the crown of her head. "What's going on?" she whispered, curling her fingers into the material of his shirt.

"It's going to be fine," Duke murmured back into her hair before addressing Renner once again. "Yeah, I'm the only one who knows the older machines, inside and out." His sigh was heavy. "I'm on my way. But only because I don't want the damn thing blowing up and putting anyone else out of a job."

Through the connection, Samantha could hear Renner's curt reply of "fine" before Duke ended the call.

"I hate to do this, but I'm needed at the factory. One of the machines—"

"Yeah." She waved off his explanation. "I got that. I'm coming with you."

"No." He looked away, but not before she saw something unsettling in his expression. Something too closely resembling dread. "The machine's been left too long and there is a small chance it could be dangerous. Even a small chance is too much where you're concerned."

"But…" Samantha realized her dress was askew, along with her hair, and she set to fixing herself. "No. No, I'll stay in the truck. We haven't finished talking yet, have we? I—"

"Sweetheart, we're nowhere *near* done." Everything in her chest seized when multiple sirens started to blare and move closer in the distance, which seemed to make Duke indecisive. Duke? Indecisive? "I need to hurry ahead. You walk back to the school, okay? Hang out with River for a while until everything is safe again. Then I'll find you."

Duke closed the gap between them, leaning down for a hard kiss. And Samantha clung to his gigantic frame, because the world seemed to be clearing into focus, just in time for everything to go to shit. *I was wrong before. This is what terrified feels like.* But she wanted Duke's concentration firmly on whatever issue needed resolving now. Not on her. "Did you hear about the knife's good-bye party?" She breathed into his neck. "Everyone was cut up about him leaving."

His bark of laughter brought the hot press of tears behind her eyes. Her arms had never felt emptier when he pulled away, heading for the office door, before stopping and turning on his booted heel. "On a scale from one to ten, how are you feeling about me?" He pounded his chest, dead center. "Right here. Right now. Don't think about it."

"Ten," she said. "*Ten.*"

He looked away, a muscle working in his cheek for a moment. Then he strode forward, tugging something out of his back pocket — a folded envelope — and handed it over. "I wasn't banking on what's inside here, you understand me? I was banking on us figuring it out *first.*" He nodded and began backing up. "But I need you to know, sweetheart. I can't go another second having you think I'd sign those papers. I wouldn't have. Not in a million years."

The blood stopped moving in her veins as Duke vanished through the doorframe, but eventually Samantha found the wherewithal to rip open the envelope. Inside, she found the annulment papers, her own signature shaky but recognizable on one of the indicated lines. But Duke's signature…it wasn't there at all. Instead, in the blunt hand she'd guessed as his that afternoon on the Art Day sign, he'd written: *Go fuck yourself.*

Samantha deflated, the envelope dropping to her thigh as tears swarmed her vision. But a clinking sound caught the developing sob in her throat. She watched through gritty eyes as a silver ring spun at her feet, a diamond winking and fading in the dull light.

I'm asking you to come live in my house, wear my ring, and be my wife. I'm asking you to try. If you're going to be scared, be scared with me.

Scared didn't even begin to cover it. Duke...her husband...could be in danger and she was standing there like a spare part. And she hadn't even given him an answer.

Samantha slipped the ring down her finger and started to run.

Chapter Nineteen

Duke angled his body so he blocked the chapel exit. Samantha looked about ready to split, but he'd gotten her this far, against all odds. So even though hell appeared to be freezing over, the deed would be done tonight. In fact, he wasn't sure if his palms were sweating because his fiancée might make a break for the door at any time. Or if moments like these were just designed to knock a man on his ass. Because that's right where he was; on his ass. Looking up at the gorgeous, complicated, and often silly-humored woman who would become his wife.

And he wondered what the hell she was thinking.

Part of him hadn't really expected her to agree. Another part, still, might even feel a little irritated that she would marry a man who'd claimed to want non-negotiable, exclusive rights to her sexual life. Had she seen right through him? Had she seen there was more? He goddamn well hoped so, otherwise she had a lot of nerve marrying him.

Duke looked down at the ring sitting in his palm. The one he'd purchased from a sidewalk vendor, after the cab let them out across the street. Shame stuck in his throat. She should have someone better. A better ring. A better offer.

"I'm sorry we don't have a decent ring."

Samantha brushed a finger over the silver band decorated with a Celtic knot. "Did you hear about the Irish woman who was disappointed in her engagement ring?"

Duke's mouth twitched. "No."

She glanced at the minister, where he sat preparing the marriage license and inserting their names into the generic cheat sheet of marriage vows. "It was a sham rock."

He shoved the ring into his pocket, took the final step toward Samantha, and drew her face close for a kiss. Against his chest, he felt the beating in her heart kick up and start to sprint, along with his own. Pumping, pounding, as their lips slid wide, tongues mating, hands finding places to grab hold of on one another's bodies.

"People usually wait until after they've been pronounced man and wife to kiss—ah, who cares," the minister droned to Duke's left.

Duke tugged away from Samantha with a growl, but she rubbed a thumb along his lower lip and settled his blood down. This was wrong. All of it. Heat crawled up the back of his neck as Samantha glanced one more time at the exit, then at him. For reassurance? Yeah…yeah, he thought that might be what she needed. And relieving her of any anxiety was what he needed.

He leaned down until his nose bumped Samantha's much smaller and more adorable one, which probably hadn't been broken twice like his. "Hey, Sam."

Her eyes crossed a little in an attempt to focus on him. "H-Hey Duke."

"We both know what's going on here."

"What does that mean?" she whispered.

Nice job, man. *"It means, when we walk out of here, we can pretend this is just about convenience or sex or paperwork. But we both know it's something else. We both know it would have*

been impossible for two people like us—who never wanted
anything serious—to end up in a chapel after one day...unless
Duke met Samantha. Okay? Not possible for either of us...
with any other person, besides each other." Please God, let me
be making sense. *"Do I need to explain any of that, or—"*

"No, I got it," she breathed.

But she didn't look toward the exit again.

• • •

The flashback to his hasty wedding to Samantha faded, along
with the glowing red exit sign, thick gray smoke obscuring
it from his vision. Waving the wafting cloud out of his face,
Duke moved through the empty factory, trying to hold on to
the feeling of having Samantha recite vows, her hands steady
in his own.

Through the fogged glass windows—which had been
installed after Renner's takeover of the factory to provide a
healthier workplace—red lights flashed, courtesy of the fire
department personnel parked outside. They'd asked him to
remain outside and wait for an emergency services unit to
arrive, but no one knew the machine like Duke. It was one
of the older pieces of equipment, installed long before the
newer, shinier machines, and it couldn't be shut off remotely.
If he'd been there when it began to overheat, he would have
opened the control panel and resolved the issue manually.

And yeah, he'd never seen the machine get to this point,
sputtering and chugging and clanging about thirty yards ahead
in the bank of smoke. The tool box he carried in his right
hand felt inadequate, but it had never felt that way before. He
could probably count on a couple fingers the times in his life
he'd been scared, and right now...yeah, he was edging along
that emotion. Two weeks ago, he wouldn't have thought twice
about entering the smoke-filled factory and doing his damn

job—hell, his sisters would miss him, but they'd have his room turned into a closet by next weekend. No, the fear threatened because…he had a wife now. Samantha was someone you stayed alive for at all costs, if only to see what she drew or said or wore next. How she kissed and chewed and saw people as characters in that beautiful, complicated mind of hers.

The machine came into view and Duke raised an eyebrow, watching the massive hunk of metal—the size of three tanks stacked on top of one another—shaking and swaying on the concrete factory floor. "Christ."

He should turn around and walk out, but if the damn thing blew, or the factory closed down for any length of time, the entire town—his friends—wouldn't have a paycheck. Maybe at first, they'd get some sort of monetary assistance, but they would dry up. They always did. Towns like Hook and the people that made them up were always forgotten eventually. But Duke wouldn't allow that. They were counting on him, even if they hadn't said anything but "be careful" as he passed them on the way into the factory, just moments earlier. He'd heard them loud and clear, though.

His grip tightened on the toolbox handle and he pushed through the increasing fog, closing his eyes and thinking of Samantha's grumpy morning face. Maybe he could install some kind of bedside coffeemaker—a safe one—that would have the caffeine hit ready when she woke up. Yeah. She'd like that.

Everything depended on her saying yes, though, didn't it? Yes, to trying. Yes, to living with his crazy family, being his wife and attempting marriage with a reformed commitment-phobe. Hopefully reforming herself in the process. He'd throw every ounce of effort into making sure it happened.

Because Duke believed in love at first sight now. And when you'd become a believer in something you'd once equated to Santa Claus, anything became possible.

He just needed to fix the damn machine first.

He reached the back panel and began muttering to it under his breath, putting on the work gloves he'd shoved in his back pocket. A good thing he did, because the surface was hot enough to melt skin off.

Saying a prayer to the gods of grease, Duke used a pair of plyers to open the back panel—

Chapter Twenty

Samantha heard the *boom* as River drove her red Pontiac
through the front factory gates. A squeal of brakes followed —
from River's car? — but Samantha barely processed the car
stopping before she got out and ran. Up ahead, the factory
itself was intact, no outer damage that she could see, but
another loud *boom*, followed by the sound of glass shattering
and smoke billowing out, told Samantha one thing. Whoever
was inside was in serious trouble.

And Duke *was* in there. She knew it deep down in her
bones that nothing would have stopped him going in and
trying to help. She'd seen the worry on his face back in the
church office and he'd already known. Already known he'd
try, no matter the cost. Unbelievable that this man had closed
himself off from the possibility of relationships for so long
when committing ran in his blood. Had he just been waiting
for her? Maybe. *Maybe.*

Anger and terror and denial rose up inside her so swiftly
she stumbled on the road, a sob wrenching from her throat.

No. *No no no.* She'd only just pulled her head out of her

ass. None of this could be real. None of it. Maybe she'd been hijacked by the Ghost of Catastrophes Future, but there still had to be time to fix everything. Right? *Right?* The ring was *there* on her finger. The giant who'd tucked it into the envelope…he'd been standing right in front of her less than twenty minutes earlier. Huge and solid and commanding and housing zero bullshit. Caring about her. Caring about *them.* Life didn't just take people like him away, did it? No, it *couldn't.*

Samantha's body jerked in shock as a fire engine screamed past. Black smoke had begun to drift down the street, sliding over cars and bystanders like waves. Everyone began to cough at once, covering their mouths with bottoms of T-shirts, but Samantha couldn't find the energy to care about something so menial as breathing. Was Duke breathing? *Was he?*

Firefighters and police officers alike were attempting to push back the crowd—most of them in coveralls, but they weren't having it.

"One of our own is in there," Samantha heard someone shout. Not just someone—it was Vaughn. River must have reached him while Samantha had been standing immobile in the street, now the blonde wrapped her arms around her husband's front, clearly trying to prevent a physical altercation with a police officer. Standing by his side was Milo, the security guard who'd walked her and Duke to Renner's officer just last week. His jaw was set as he spoke in a low voice to a firefighter, but the man only shook his head.

"We have a crew moving in through the back. If he's alive—"

That's when Samantha stopped listening and her ears began to ring. She moved through the cloud of gray like a zombie.

"On a scale from one to ten, how you feeling about me?" He pounded his chest, dead center. *"Right here. Right now.*

Don't think about it."

"Ten," she said. "Ten."

Tears fell in hot waterfalls down Samantha's face. Why hadn't she said eleven, dammit? Could she go back in time and say eleven?

Her feet continued to move without a direct command. The sword she'd swallowed made her whole body feel stiff, sharp pain slicing straight up to her jugular. *He can't die. He can't die. He's too big.* It was a stupid refrain but continued to loop back and replay nonetheless, layered with images of him painting faces and barbequing. His strong hands on her ankles when she sat on his shoulders at the concert. Oh God, he'd thrown an Art Day in her honor. To win her back. And she'd balked? Actually balked? The sword in her chest twisted.

Someone touched Samantha's arm and she turned her head, seeing Renner through a daze. It cleared, however, almost immediately, to be replaced by white hot rage. "How could you let him go in there?"

Fatigue etched itself around his eyes. "No one could stop him, Samantha."

An anguished noise broke free at the vision of Duke ignoring warnings and muscling his way through, determination written on his hard features. "This wouldn't have happened if you hadn't fired him," she choked out. "God, I hate you right now."

"Get in line."

Samantha had never struck another soul in her life, but nothing could keep her pulling back a bunched fist and sailing it in her brother's direction—her arm was caught in midair, however, stealing the building promise of satisfaction. She turned her head to find Milo was the culprit and the next target for her anger, but the deep sympathy in his expression split her wrath down the center. Through the cracks poured such thick, awful grief, her legs would no longer support her.

"I'm sorry," Milo said, his voice like gravel. "Not about Duke. Not yet, anyway. That man is indestructible." He flicked a glance at Renner. "I'm sorry I can't let you hit your brother. I'm paid to protect the factory and he's part of it." While sauntering away, Milo threw a look over his shoulder. "Not that it wouldn't do him some good."

Milo walked away before she could question that statement. Samantha wanted him to come back and say more things that would give her hope—false or not—about Duke, but the sound of groaning metal rent the air. A waft of smoke poured out from the side entrance of the factory, but she could barely see through the gray haze filling her surroundings. Everyone moved in that direction at once, faster when the sound of boots hitting pavement could be heard.

Even knowing it could be the firemen who'd gone in to find Duke, Samantha ran, weaving through the crowd of factory workers, all of whom were eerily silent. So much *silence*. Or maybe her ears had blocked out everything but the high-pitched ringing that had returned with a vengeance. When she cleared the group, a patch of gray cleared long enough for her to make out five figures. Desperate to get closer but hindered by the police officers, Samantha crammed her fingers against her mouth and waited. Waited. The longest seconds of her life.

And then Duke walked out through the smoke, a portable oxygen mask pressed to his face. *Oh, thank God, thank God, thank God.* An image of him sliding on a pair of aviators and giving a cocky salute, like the star of an action movie, sketched itself on the page of her mind before sliding away into a cool ocean of relief.

The cheer that went up around Samantha was deafening, but the roar in her heart drowned it out. Duke was covered in soot, his T-shirt ripped at the collar, his limp more noticeable than usual. Blood. There was blood on his arms, cheek, and jeans, but he was alive. Duke was alive. Even as he brushed off the firefighter's attempts to aid him in walking, he looked right at Samantha. And crooked his finger.

With the police distracted by the crowd's rowdy celebration, Samantha slipped between the officers and sprinted toward her husband. She could barely see through the unshed tears in her eyes, but there was no missing Duke. He was larger than life with his arms wide open to receive her. She wanted to jump and climb his sturdy body, but not knowing his injuries, she threw her arms around his waist instead, letting loose a watery sob.

Duke dropped the oxygen mask and picked her up anyway.

The firemen that had accompanied him from the building were met by paramedics with oxygen masks. "Lucky man," Samantha heard one of them mutter. "He was thrown by the blast, but the machine's control panel shielded him from the worst of it."

The close call had Samantha's breath shuddering out, her arms tightening.

"Sam." One hand twisted in her hair. "Give me an answer, sweetheart. Give me what I lived for."

"Yes. *Yes*, I'll stay married to you. I'm already wearing the ring." Her words were muffled by his chest, but he must have heard them, because he staggered back and sat down, right on the concrete, Samantha still clinging to him like she'd never let go. "We'll do it right, too. I'll live in your gorgeous house and barbeque on Saturdays. I'm sorry. I'm so sorry I let you leave without an answer. Oh God, you could have…you—"

"I want the pastor," Duke shouted, silencing the cheering that still went on around them. "Someone get the pastor. *Now*."

Samantha turned her head long enough to watch three

men hightail it down the block, presumably to do Duke's bidding. "Why do we need a pastor? We're already married."

A paramedic approached. "Sir, we need to take a look at your injurie—"

"Nope." Duke clasped the sides of Samantha's face in his big hands. "We're doing this right. We're saying the words with our eyes open, no question how we feel. Or why we're making promises to each other. We're becoming husband and wife because there's some heavy magic here between us and we're not questioning it. Ever again. We're letting the magic work." He picked up her hand, brushing his lips over the ring she wore on her finger. "Will you marry me again, Samantha?"

She laid a kiss on him that turned up the volume of the crowd's cheers. "Yes."

"I wouldn't mind giving her away," another voice said behind them. Renner. Samantha smiled in relief against Duke's mouth, turning to find Renner standing stiffly, hands in his suit jacket's pockets. "Someone should. Someone who has a hard time admitting he was wrong. In this one case. Maybe."

Duke reached out a soot-covered hand and Renner shook it. "We'd like that."

And ten minutes later when the pastor arrived, Duke and Samantha said their vows in the settling smoke, without a single hesitation.

Epilogue

Two months later

Samantha had turned the basement of Duke's house into her studio. Although, according to Duke, it was *their* house. She was still getting used to referring to it as such, but was steadily growing addicted to the way he smiled every time she remembered.

"Our house," she murmured, a little thrill tingling in her veins. "*Our* house."

Not only did it belong to them, but also to his four sisters, who by Samantha's stubborn decree were not allowed to move out. Not until they were ready, anyway. So they'd plugged her into the hair dryer schedule and added another place setting to the table. Right next to Duke, obviously. And more often than not, she ended up sitting on his lap, usually greeted by a round of sighs so gusty they blew her hair right back.

It was awesome.

Samantha turned in a circle and admired the studio that was finally beginning to feel complete. Upon her moving in—also known as the day of the factory explosion—Duke had been worried she would feel claustrophobic living with so many people. So one afternoon while she'd been packing up the remainder of her things in the city, he'd cleaned the basement floor to ceiling. Then the following week, he'd tapped some of his factory buddies to help install hardwood flooring, put up drywall and paint. Of course, Samantha had immediately ruined that paint job with tiny pinholes, hanging her various sketches of Duke's many characters on every available inch of space. But he hadn't seemed to mind.

A secret smile curved Samantha's lips when she remembered how they'd made love on her new desk, the piece of furniture bumping against the basement wall, Duke's choked curses warming her neck. Yes, he'd definitely approved of her décor choice.

Upstairs, she heard the house's front door open and shut, signaling Duke's return from an overtime shift at the factory. He'd been working late since the explosion, returning the factory to working condition so none of his coworkers would spend a single day unemployed. Just one of the many reasons she adored her husband.

Her husband. Who would have believed she could say those words without having a seizure, let alone swooning so hard little hearts *bloop-blooped* in the air around her head? Their first two weeks living together, they'd done their best going slow, probably afraid to overwhelm one another. In bed, there'd been no pretense of politeness. Oh, no. But outside, they'd been almost shy around one another. Until Duke had finally shown up at her job in Manhattan one afternoon, kissed the hell out of her right there at her desk, and said, "Just in case you needed a reminder that I'm all in. Or that I can't imagine my life without you anymore. Take your pick."

"I'll take both," she'd whispered. "And I'm all in, too."

Knowing the basement would be Duke's first stop after

he removed his boots, Samantha hopped up on the desk and fluffed her hair. She'd been working all day on the Art on Wheels launch set to take place next summer, not to mention making travel arrangements for her and Duke. Starting soon, they would begin traveling with Renner on occasional business trips where he thought their united front would be beneficial. Thankfully, the relationship between her brother and Duke had gone from combative to respectful almost overnight. While Duke had explained he would bury any hatchet—great or small—to make Samantha happy, she'd been surprised by Renner's immediate change of heart. He'd been acting a touch out of character lately, and she couldn't seem to shake the feeling that it had something to do with Milo Bautista.

She'd have to keep an eye on that. An interested one.

The basement door flung open and rebounded off the wall, sending Samantha's hearts ricocheting around her ribs. Man oh man, her husband liked to make an entrance. There he stood, huge and hearty in the doorframe, remnants of grease on the collar of his tight white T-shirt and faded work jeans. "There's my sweetheart."

"Here I am," she said, her voice already smoky in anticipation of touching him, being with him, talking to him. "How was your day?"

"Incomplete until right now."

He eliminated the distance between them, closed his work-roughened hands around her knees and dropped a sweet kiss on her mouth. Sweet at first, anyway. The passion that swept in was unavoidable and neither one of them tried. Samantha's head fell back and Duke pressed his advantage, marrying their tongues while his hands massaged her knees, opening them wider on the desk.

When he broke the kiss, Samantha reached for his shoulders, intending to drag him back, but the look on his face gave her pause. "What?"

"There was a new drawing on the wall when I walked in."

Pleasure stole through her limbs like melted wax. "There are over fifty sketches and you can tell when one is different?"

"That's right." His fingertips trailed up and down the insides of her thighs. "It's on the outer right edge."

Samantha's heart rode an elevator up to her throat and stayed there. She'd been preparing for this moment all day, thinking she would be nervous, but now that it had arrived, *ready* didn't even begin to describe how anxious she was. No, there was excitement and a sense of coming full circle. But no nerves. There wasn't room for a single one with this man standing there, anchoring her. Loving her.

He'd told her how much. Several times. But she hadn't said the same back just yet, had she? Even though she swore she'd been feeling it forever.

"Go look," she breathed, nudging his chest with the heel of her hand.

Duke's perceptive eyes narrowed as he backed away, turning toward the Duke Wall of Fame. She'd spent so much time trying to decide which persona fit him best. Sea captain, gladiator, super hero. Celebrity chef, werewolf, soldier, action movie hero. It turned out Duke was all of them and more.

Pressing the back of her hand over her mouth, Samantha watched as Duke found the new sketch. It was larger than the others, out of necessity. Inside the giant bubble letters L-O-V-E she'd simply drawn as many Duke personas as she could fit, keeping them inside the confines of the word, same as he filled up every inch of her heart.

When Duke looked back at her, his own heart was there in his eyes, huge and bottomless, the impact of it robbing her of breath.

"I love you," Samantha said, her voice uneven. "I love my husband. I could fill a thousand sketchpads and still never find

a description for you. Because there isn't one. You're just…
love. And you have mine."

He reached her in one giant stride and crushed her against
his chest. "You have mine, too, Sam." One big hand tunneled
into her hair to cradle her head. "You have it forever. My wife.
I love my wife."

When Duke carried Samantha upstairs a few minutes
later, cradling her against his chest like a long-lost treasure,
four smiling sisters removed two place settings from the table
without comment…and started making cash bets on when
they'd finally have a niece or nephew to spoil.

Acknowledgments

Thank you to…

My husband, Patrick, and daughter, Mackenzie, for their patience and love. My editor, Heather Howland for her insight and encouragement. Sara Eirew, for the amazing cover photograph. Eagle, for her beta reading prowess. Nelle, for continuing to love the books and ask why they're not in her inbox. The Babes, as always, for making me laugh all throughout the day. Thank you!

About the Author

New York Times and USA TODAY bestselling author Tessa Bailey lives in Brooklyn, New York, with her husband and young daughter. When she isn't writing or reading romance, she enjoys a good argument and thirty-minute recipes.

www.tessabailey.com
Join Bailey's Babes!

RAW REDEMPTION

BOILING POINT

OWNED BY FATE

EXPOSED BY FATE

DRIVEN BY FATE

If you love sexy romance, one-click these steamy Brazen releases…

EMERGENCY ATTRACTION
a *Love Emergency* novel by Samanthe Beck

When Shane Maguire escaped to the Marines ten years ago, he only regretted one thing–leaving Sinclair Smith behind. But now he's back, and determined to reclaim the girl who got away. But it's been a long time. Sinclair isn't ready to risk everything on a bad boy who breaks promises. Even though she'd really, really like to…

FALLING FOR THE BAD GIRL
a *Cutting Loose* novel by Nina Croft

Detective Nathan Carter is a cop, through and through. But his work ethic—and libido—are thrown off balance when he heads up the case against jewel thief, Regan Malloy. Because with one sizzling look, she's had him hot and hard ever since. But now Regan's out of prison and hoping to start over. It's inevitable that they'll meet up again—in bars, hotels…and hotel beds. Still, it's just desire. If they give it enough time, it'll burn itself out. Because a good boy and a bad girl can't possibly make it work. Or can they?

Taking a Shot
a Montana Wolfpack novel by Taryn Leigh Taylor

Hockey star Brett Sillinger's never been afraid of a little trouble. But when his personal life ends up in the tabloids, he knows his career is on thin ice. Luckily, a new team decides to take a chance on him. All he has to do is keep head in the game. But when Chelsea London, the owner's daughter walks in, looking for one night of nameless, no-strings passion, well, what's a guy to do?

Leveling the Field
a *Gamers* novel by Megan Erickson

Reclusive gaming magazine exec Ethan Talley is furious when his business partner hires a photographer—a *gorgeous* photographer with an affinity for glitter and sex—to take pictures for the newspaper. No matter how badly he wants the woman… under him, over him, against the nearest wall…he has reasons for not wanting to be on camera anymore, and his scars are only one of them.

Made in United States
Troutdale, OR
06/03/2024

20311196R00141